Kevin Branigan, the "cra... *Bittersweet Harvest* and *Still* ... bachelor. But with Erin O'Connor, he'd more than met his match!

"Erin, Have You Ever Been At A Loss For Words?"

Kevin asked as she passed him.

"Not yet. Thanks for folding my laundry."

Kevin cleared his throat. "I didn't know you'd hung it out there this morning—we have a dryer."

"Heat ruins the elastic in my underwear. Besides it didn't rain." She looked at his expression. "Your brother and his wife hang theirs out."

"They're married."

"Married! You and I have to be married before I can hang my camisole next to your shorts? I thought you'd be pleased that I'm doing my share of the chores."

"My bachelor brothers were pleased. I'll say that."

She began to laugh. "You've been teased! I thought you commanded too much respect for that. Next time I'll string them up here in the bedroom so no one will notice."

"I'll notice," he said under his breath.

"I'd like that," she replied, no louder than he.

"Erin! Occasionally a man, even a man of few words, likes to have the last one."

Dear Reader:

Series and Spin-offs! Connecting characters and intriguing interconnections to make your head whirl.

In Joan Hohl's successful trilogy for Silhouette Desire—*Texas Gold* (7/86), *California Copper* (10/86), *Nevada Silver* (1/87)—Joan created a cast of characters that just wouldn't quit. You figure out how *Lady Ice* (5/87) connects. And in August, "J.B." demanded his own story—*One Tough Hombre*. In *Falcon's Flight*, coming in November, you'll learn *all* about . . .?

Annette Broadrick's *Return to Yesterday* (6/87) introduced Adam St. Clair. This August *Adam's Story* tells about the woman who saves his life—and teaches him a thing or two about love!

The six Branigan brothers appeared in Leslie Davis Guccione's *Bittersweet Harvest* (10/86) and *Still Waters* (5/87). September brings *Something in Common*, where the eldest of the strapping Irishmen finds love in unexpected places.

Midnight Rambler by Linda Barlow is in October—a special Halloween surprise, and totally unconnected to anything.

Keep an eye out for other Silhouette Desire favorites—Diana Palmer, Dixie Browning, Ann Major and Elizabeth Lowell, to name a few. You never know when secondary characters will insist on their own story. . . .

All the best,

Isabel Swift
Senior Editor & Editorial Coordinator
Silhouette Books

LESLIE DAVIS GUCCIONE
Something in Common

Silhouette Desire

Published by Silhouette Books New York

America's Publisher of Contemporary Romance

With love to
Tucker Warriner, Katherine Beers Hazzard
and, of course, Joe
because Real Life started on Marlborough Street

SILHOUETTE BOOKS
300 East 42nd St., New York, N.Y. 10017

Copyright © 1987 by Leslie Davis Guccione

ISBN: 0-373-05376-2

First Silhouette Books printing September 1987

All the characters in this book are fictitious. Any
resemblance to actual persons, living or dead, is
purely coincidental.

America's Publisher of Contemporary Romance

Printed in the U.S.A.

LESLIE DAVIS GUCCIONE

lives with her husband and three children in a state of semichaos in a historical sea captains' district south of Boston. When she's not at her typewriter, she's actively researching everything from sailboats to cranberry bogs. What free time she has is spent sailing and restoring her circa 1827 Cape Cod cottage. Her ideas for her books are based on the world around her. As she states, "Romance is right under your nose." She has also written under the name Leslie Davis.

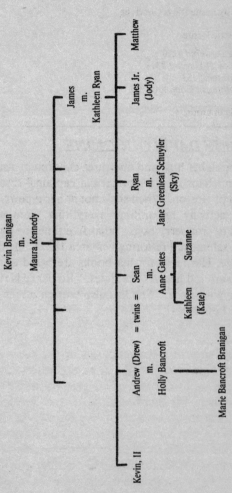

BRANIGAN FAMILY TREE

Kevin Branigan
m.
Maura Kennedy

Kevin, II

Andrew (Drew) = twins = Sean
m.   m.
Holly Bancroft   Anne Gates

Marie Bancroft Branigan

Kathleen
(Kate)

Suzanne

James
m.
Kathleen Ryan

Ryan
m.
Jane Greenleaf Schuyler
(Sky)

James Jr.
(Jody)

Matthew

One

It began with the simplest of gestures. She tilted her head to look up at his face as she offered her hand. "You must be the heir apparent, *Kevin* Branigan."

He laughed and watched the candlelight play in her copper-colored hair. "And you could only be Erin O'Connor, the nurse helping Nancy and my kid brother survive medical school."

"They burn the midnight oil, I keep the home fires burning. The three of us are like ships in the night most of the time," she replied, aware of the warm pressure of his fingers over hers. She was having the time of her twenty-four-year-old life that New Year's Eve, flirting with five of the handsomest brothers south of Boston. She and college friend Nancy Reed shared a Back Bay apartment with the sixth. Nancy and Matthew Branigan were third-year Harvard Medical School students and it was Matt who had included Erin and Nancy in his family's New Year's Eve celebration. The private party at Santé, a Plymouth restaurant, was Erin's introduction to Kevin, who had raised Matt and the four brothers in between.

Wits were sharp, humor intact. Without exception they all lived up to their extraordinary reputations. The fact that they were nearly equal in height, six feet to a few inches more, and dressed similarly in dark blazers and dress slacks enhanced Erin's impression of solidarity. The Branigan jawline was strong, their chins square; their Black Irish coloring began with thick, dark hair, and ended with light eyes, going from blue to hazel.

They ranged in age from twenty-five to thirty-seven. Matt, the youngest, would be a physician, and twenty-eight-year-old Jody was a lawyer. They were both obvious sources of pride to the other four who had made their education possible. The Branigans had been orphaned for twenty years, thrusting head-of-the-household status on Kevin at only seventeen. Even now Erin noticed the ways in which his brothers deferred to him.

She laughed at the jokes about Matt and his penchant for living with women after a lifetime of a masculine household. She entertained them with stories of hospital life. That they accepted her warmly and readily was a testament to Matt's glowing opinion of her, as well as her lively personality. Matthew Branigan was everything she would have wanted in a brother, and the fact that there were five more at home was heady stuff to the oldest of three sisters.

Sean and Drew, the identical twins, were both happily married. Sean married his high school sweetheart and Drew had swept Holly Bancroft off her feet when she'd come from Philadelphia to sell off the neighboring bogs she'd inherited. She was now eight months pregnant and freely admitting to Erin that she was still adjusting to the abrupt changes in her life.

Ryan, the thirty-one-year-old middle brother, arrived with Jane "Sky" Schuyler, who looked every inch the heiress she was. Jody had come stag and Kevin had a statuesque brunette named Claudia on his arm. Erin watched the men with the curiosity that came from her professional interest in genetics and Matt's endless stories about each of them. She watched the women with amusement. She and Nancy were the only ones in their twenties.

Erin's fresh, open features were accentuated by wide brown eyes and a spectacular head of thick, coppery hair, shimmering with strawberry highlights. As an obstetrical nurse, she kept it bound most of the time so that on evenings like these, she enjoyed letting it tumble onto her shoulders. Physically she fit somewhere between the cheerleader freshness of Sean's wife Anne and the serene prettiness of expectant Holly. Claudia's overt sexiness and Sky's flawless, aristocratic beauty were out of her league altogether.

It was a mix that made for lively conversation from cranberries to breast-feeding and childbirth training. Medicine held its own since Sean, a fire fighter, and Ryan, a part-time police officer, were emergency medical technicians. Fraternal rumbling between Ryan and Kevin sparked an occasional conversation, heightening Erin's sense of family. During the long, relaxed hours she was one of them, and it felt like a home away from home.

At midnight she stood on tiptoe six times to stretch her five-foot-five-inch frame for a kiss. "I'm making the rounds in chronological order so I can keep all of you straight," she told Matt as she pivoted to Jody. After five quick kisses and hugs, she had eased her way to the corner table.

Kevin turned from Claudia and held his champagne glass aside. "I thought you'd never get here," he said with a laugh. "Have you figured out one from the other?"

"My goodness, there are certainly a lot of you," she replied, rising for the last time onto her toes. She closed her eyes and he kissed her, briefly resting his hand at the back of her head. Her scalp tingled and her heart jumped beneath her simple wool sheath. Erin opened her eyes. Kevin's were wide and very blue. He looked almost startled as she stood close enough to see the gray in his temples. "Happy New Year," she said breathlessly.

Five months later Erin was commenting on her impression of Sky Schuyler that night. She and Ryan were the only Branigan couple Erin had seen since New Year's. Holly had survived an emergency mid-winter delivery and it was Ryan who had brought the baby into the world. Erin chatted about the birth with Matt as she scooted herself onto her oak table in the dining alcove of their apartment. She was trying to put Matt at ease as she began to unbutton her nurse's uniform.

"Erin, you don't have to do this."

"Matt, you're about to begin your Obstetrics and Gynecology rotation, and you're a wreck over breast exams. I *teach* this stuff for heaven's sake! I'm sure admitting you're nervous was the hard part. But you need the practice and I've got the mammaries, meager though they may be." She took the hand towel he thrust at her and covered her cleavage.

"You're a sweetheart to do this," he muttered as she lay down.

"Consider it a professional courtesy. I only wish Nancy weren't doing her pediatrics in London. I'm sure she'd agree that we can't have a Harvard man with sweaty palms." She lifted the right side of the towel and put her open hand up under the back of her head as he began the professional probing. She thought better of kidding him any more about the women in his life who'd volunteer; it would only embarrass him further.

When Matt had finished the exam, she sat up. "I knew you'd do fine. Before I change, would you like me to show you where the ducts can clog in nursing mothers?"

Matt shook his head. "Any more of this and your virtue's at stake. Hugh O'Connor would have my head, as it is."

Erin smiled. "My father thinks you're a built-in security guard. If he only knew you spent most of your time at the hospital." She started down the hall toward her bedroom with the towel at her breasts and called as an afterthought, "I got a call from the head of the department."

Matt turned around. "No kidding! Did you get the consultation?"

She nodded. "My first crack at administration. They want me to review the programs under Women's Services at Sky's clinic. I'm being loaned out for a week. I get to bring a little Harvard expertise to Millbrook."

"Go put some clothes on and tell me about it at dinner," he called.

Through a string of events begun with Ryan's Police League work with delinquent boys, Sky was volunteering at the Millbrook Medical Clinic. They were in the process of pulling funding together for a Women's Services department and Erin suggested her own facility in Boston as a model program. Matt's hometown would be getting a full-fledged program of its own for pregnant and lactating women.

"Of course you'll stay at the house while you're in Millbrook," Matt said when she'd changed into jeans and they sat down to spaghetti.

Erin raised her eyebrows. "The house, your house at the bogs? Matt, there's no need for me to impose, it's close enough for me to commute."

"Over an hour each way," he scoffed. "Kevin's rambling around in it all by himself now. He could use the company and he'd keep an eye on you while you're down there. Sean and Anne don't have the room, Drew and Holly have the baby and Sky's entire second floor's being restored."

"I could stay with Jody in Plymouth." She was teasing, but the thought of a week alone with the head of the clan had caused a tightening in every muscle in her stomach. She saw Kevin through Matt's eyes, the no-nonsense rock they all leaned on. If the youngest brother painted the oldest as larger than life, Erin's one evening with him New Year's Eve had only enhanced the opinion.

"I don't trust Jody; besides he's got a *one* bedroom condo," Matt was saying.

Matt's words brought her attention back. "I'm sure Kevin likes his privacy. You're always telling me how he loves being alone for the first time since your parents died, you know, having nobody to wait up for."

Matt had cocked his head. "Are you intimidated by my oldest brother?"

"Of course not," she insisted.

"Well, good. Because Kevin's just what Hugh O'Connor ordered to keep you out of harm's way."

Erin pointed a bread stick at him. "Matthew, my father doesn't require that a man monitor my entire existence beyond the boundaries of our dairy farm."

He grinned. "That's what you think."

She shook her head and teased, "Kevin happens to be gorgeous and eligible. What makes you think I won't come back seduced and starry-eyed?"

Matt laughed, the idea clearly ridiculous. "Kevin's thirty-seven! He's a confirmed bachelor who likes his work and his dogs and his women, in that order. He's been thriving out there on those bogs since he was a kid. More to the point, he wouldn't think of you as anything more than his kid brother's roommate, dewy-eyed though you may be."

"Thanks a lot."

He mussed her hair. "It's a compliment. I wouldn't let you near him if I thought anything else. You're too career-oriented. You need somebody with charm and education. You'll find yourself a Harvard man and spend the rest of your life discussing postpartum depression and infant bonding."

"How depressing," she muttered.

They got up and cleared the table together. "Besides," he added, "his taste in women runs to the older-and-wiser type with big—"

"Matthew," she interrupted, "you've made your point."

They were distracted by the phone and an impromptu lunch invitation from Sky who was at her family's Beacon Hill house. Matt declined immediately. "I finish my Orthopedic rotation tomorrow, but Erin needs the break." Erin agreed as she went back to the kitchen and the dishes, leaving Matt to tell Sky of the consultation appointment.

A half hour later the roommates parted company, Matt to the hospital and Erin to the bathtub, where she took advantage of the rare opportunity to soak without anyone anxious to use the facilities. The apartment was quiet, filled only with distant street noise through the open windows. When her hair was dry and she'd pulled on a cotton night-gown, she wrote Nancy a letter, envious of her time in London but not the studies. They'd been friends all through college, but where Nancy had pursued medical school, Erin opted for graduate school in nursing. It was dark when she sealed the letter and she looked at the distant lights of Cambridge twinkling on the far shore of the Charles River, letting the light breeze from the window ruffle her hair.

She wasn't looking forward to her first summer in the city if this Friday night in June was any indication. She turned off all but a small lamp for Matt and went to bed, wondering how Millbrook would compare to the rolling farmland she'd left behind in northwestern New Jersey. In the apartment below, a Boston Conservatory student practiced and Erin fell asleep lulled by the strains of Chopin.

Long after midnight, three raps on her bedroom door acknowledged that Matt was home and when she told him to come in, he pushed open the door and stood in the shadows. "Patients all right?" she asked.

"I'm leaving them in good hands," he replied, "and speaking of hands, thanks again for the practice, you were a doll to do that for me."

"That's what roommates are for, Harvard."

He laughed and turned to leave when she added, "You're going to make a wonderful doctor, you know."

He hesitated before he spoke. "Coming from you, it means a lot."

"Sleep well," she replied and settled back into the pillow.

Erin managed to get some breakfast into Matt before he left for the hospital Saturday morning. She enjoyed fussing over Nancy and Matt, helping to ease their frantic schedules. She thought about them both as she walked across Back Bay to Beacon Hill. There was enough breeze off the Charles River to keep the June weather comfortable and she studied the window boxes and spring plantings as she went. At the end of Marlborough Street she skirted the Public Garden. *A week as the houseguest of Kevin Branigan.* Erin took a deep breath to calm her heartbeat as her seersucker dress billowed around her legs and her hair snapped across her face. She had to keep reminding herself that it had only been an impersonal kiss on New Year's Eve.

The hill began in earnest at the corner of Charles and Mt. Vernon and Erin climbed. Sky might have an opinion about what to do. Matt was right that an invitation to Schuyler House was impossible. The Millbrook antique was in the throes of restoration. Erin had to laugh at herself. Here she was, unbuttoning her uniform to help Matt be a better medical student, yet too intimidated to consider a week as a simple houseguest in a house big enough to have held six boys. Kevin was probably no different from his youngest brother, just older.

A clump of tourists parted as Erin reached number eighty-five Mt. Vernon Street, as impressive as Sky herself. She knocked at the family manse and gazed at the balustrade while she waited.

Staying in Millbrook instead of commuting every day would give her time to do the paperwork, put her feet up, and study the community as well as the clinic. Professionally it made sense. Emotionally it did, too. She'd mention it to Sky. Second opinions were worthwhile in more fields than medicine.

The wide door began to open and Erin smiled even as her heart jumped again. Kevin Branigan stood before her and invited her in.

Two

Erin raised her finger. "Don't tell me—Kevin, the cranberry baron."

"You *were* able to tell us apart, after all," he said as she moved past him into the foyer.

"This is a nice surprise. What brings you to Boston?"

"The Red Sox. Ryan and I came up for a game last night."

"They won, I think."

"Sure did." He was dressed far more informally than New Year's Eve, but he looked as authoritative in the daylight as he had in the darkened restaurant. Erin chided herself that a handsome man wearing a simple polo shirt and khakis should play such havoc with her respiratory system.

"You know Matt has that article about you from the *Wall Street Journal* tacked on our refrigerator," she offered as she followed him through the foyer to the front parlor.

"Don't believe everything you read," he replied.

"If the crown fits, you might as well wear it," she answered, enjoying the sound of his deep laugh. Sky and Ryan turned to greet her and she was struck, as always, by the physical perfection of the couple. The housekeeper appeared with a tray of tulip-shaped glasses and Erin realized Kevin was pulling a bottle of champagne from an ice bucket.

"We've been waiting for you," Sky said. "I'm just sorry Matt couldn't make it."

Kevin filled the four glasses and Ryan raised his. "It occurred to me at breakfast that if I'm going to aspire to all of this, it would be a whole lot easier to marry it than to break my back trying to earn it."

Erin gasped softly and caught Kevin's eye, but Sky spoke. "Once you've fallen in love with the town terror, the rest pale by comparison. I'm just sorry it took thirteen years for that to sink in."

"You're engaged!" Erin cried. "Fantastic. This all started up again New Year's Eve, didn't it? A toast!" They sipped and she smiled over her glass at Kevin. "Your brothers are dropping like flies."

Kevin shook his head slowly, a bemused expression making his blue eyes bright. Ryan raised his glass again. "Here's to the first chaperon we ever had."

"And the man who drove me home to my father," Sky added.

"Separating you two was like scraping filings from a magnet," Kevin replied. "Thank God that stage of my life is over."

Ryan raised his glass again. "Since I'm the last man to move out of the house, I should propose a toast to Kevin and his new freedom. Alone at last! For some, I guess, life does begin at forty."

Kevin grimaced. "Thirty-seven, if you don't mind. You two have my blessing just as long as you don't run off on a honeymoon in the midst of the harvest. I spent the last year convincing you to give up police work, Ryan. I'll be damned if I lose you to some tropical paradise." The brothers eyed each other good-naturedly and then Kevin turned to his future sister-in-law. "As long as you're around, I've got no need to worry. You're my insurance, Sky. You've always been the gold at the end of Ryan's rainbow."

Sky kissed his cheek. "*Now* I win his approval," she told Erin. "You can't imagine what it was like trying to sneak around with Ryan when we were eighteen and Kevin was twenty-four going on fifty. He had a look that would stop you in your tracks. Mr. Responsibility!"

"Somebody had to protect your reputation," Kevin said.

Sky laughed. "A little tarnish has been good for my character. And now that all you Branigans have made it safely to the adult world, Kevin, it's your turn to let loose." She suddenly turned to Erin. "I almost forgot. Letting loose will have to wait. Erin's coming to the clinic for a week and Matt wants her to stay at the house."

"My house," Kevin said without inflection.

Erin flushed as the three of them looked at her. Kevin's eyes were wide and piercing blue. When she looked at him, she got a sense of what Sky must have felt as a teenager. He looked at her pink cheeks, her hair and back to her eyes. Sky was explaining Matt's request from their phone call the previous night. "I think another toast is in order, one to Erin. Millbrook's about to get its first Harvard consultant." They all sipped.

"There's no reason why I can't commute down and back," Erin replied as she put her empty glass on the coffee table. "Matt's far too presumptuous."

"Matt knows you'd be welcome," Kevin said.

They went into lunch, served at one end of the gleaming, mahogany table set simply, but impeccably, for four. Over chicken salad and a Pinot blanc from the wine cellar they talked Red Sox, house restoration, life with Matt and summer in Millbrook.

"The pace slows some," Kevin said, "which is why we're catching up on repairs. We overhauled the barn this winter, the roof's being done now. Drew and Holly have put in a new sprinkler system and we updated ours. But the ditches need cleaning, bogs need weeding. You're not likely to see a lot of me, anyway, so there's no need to feel like you're imposing."

His Yankee forthrightness made Erin blink. It seemed obvious to her that she was being put at arm's length. He spoke the way a surgeon might, outlining a procedure. The expression on his handsome face was guarded and she wondered whether he expected her to outline her own schedule. "You make it sound as though there'll barely be time for a wedding," she replied.

"There better be," Ryan said. "If my Bronco stays in the Schuyler House driveway much longer without one, I'll scandalize Millbrook all over again."

Sky laughed. "You can't get away with much when your house sits smack dab in the middle of the main drag. Kevin, on the other hand, could be doing all kinds of scandalous things out there on the bogs with no one the wiser except a brother or two."

"My time is my own," he said over a last bite of chicken. Erin made a point to keep that in mind.

After lunch the men settled in the library to watch another baseball game and Sky and Erin moved into the parlor to talk about the clinic.

"I never would have gotten into this volunteer program if it hadn't been for Ryan," Sky said. "He and Kevin still argue about the time Ryan puts in with the boys from the Police League, but he really makes a difference in their lives,

I think. He's got a group of teenagers he drags around with him. They're going to paint the trim on my carriage barn. They got underfoot all winter out at Kevin's barn where Ryan had them working on car engines. They were arguing about it New Year's Eve, as I recall.''

"Kevin can be intimidating," Erin said.

"Kevin? He thought he had to be for so many years; I think it got to be a habit. I'm sure Matt's told you that their neighbor, Peter Bancroft, and Kevin took over completely when the boys lost their parents. Underneath he's just doing what he thinks is best for his brothers. A doctor, an attorney, a former police officer, a fire fighter and a thriving cranberry business—Kevin deserves a lot of credit.''

Their conversation drifted to wedding plans, an engagement party and Sky's family. It was nearly five o'clock when Ryan and Kevin appeared at the door and Erin looked at her watch. She stood up and thanked them all, joking that the walk home would burn off the luncheon calories.

"I'll drive you home," Kevin said.

Erin shook her head and tried to swallow her surprise. "Thank you, but it's a lovely walk. I'll be fine."

"Matt'll have my head on a platter if I let you do that," he said, beginning to grin at her defiance.

The flaming hair slid off her shoulders as she threw her head back and looked up into his face. "Matthew seems to think he's got some secret pact with my father. I'm perfectly capable of getting home safely."

"I'll see her home," Kevin said to Ryan and Sky.

"Kevin..."

"A little chivalry's good for the soul, yours and mine."

Erin gave Sky a pleading look but it was met with a shrug. "One's as bad as another, you might as well relax and enjoy it. Kevin could use the cultural tour, anyway. His idea of a Boston landmark is a box seat at Fenway Park."

"Ready?" He opened the door, smiling at Sky's comment.

When the door had closed behind them, Erin's heart resumed its erratic thumping. Silly, she chided herself. She felt not unlike she did her first night as head of a childbirth class with the chief of OB/GYN in the back of the room.

Kevin shoved his hands into his pockets and change rattled pleasantly in lieu of conversation. She made it as far as the sidewalk. "If you'd rather, you can just walk me down the hill to the subway. The Green Line goes right to Copley Square."

Kevin paused on the cobblestones. "Would you rather ride? I've got my car right in the back."

"Really? Well, yes, maybe, if that's what you want. It wouldn't take as long. I can walk anytime."

"Erin!"

He startled her and she pressed her hand over her heart. "What?"

"If I were Matt or Sky how would you *want* to get home?"

"Matt or Sky, why do you ask?" She put her hand from her breast to her cheek. "Oh, you think I'm intimidated. I *am* being a little dippy, aren't I?"

"A little," he murmured.

She sighed and shook back her hair. "Well, I don't want you to feel obligated. Matt is terribly overprotective and I feel guilty that I'm taking up your time. I'd like to walk. It's a beautiful evening in a city I love."

"Then it's settled." He started off with Erin beside him, down the hill. The regal houses of Louisburg Square caught their attention and they watched the low sun glint off a granite stoop and the iron fencing. A nun in a lightweight gray habit smiled and nodded as she passed them and turned onto the most exclusive street in the old section of Boston.

"Episcopal, did you know that?"

Kevin looked from one woman to the other. "Excuse me?"

"The Episcopalian Order of the Sisters of St. Margaret have a convent on the corner, right here on the Hill. You see them once in a while. I haven't seen a Catholic sister in a habit in years, have you?"

Kevin looked puzzled. "I don't know. No, I guess I haven't; then again, I haven't been looking." He was quiet again and they reached Charles Street without conversation. He took his hand from his pocket and touched the small of her back as they crossed the busy intersection at Beacon Street. The silence seemed louder than the traffic and Erin concentrated on the pleasant warmth emanating from his hand.

She looked across the street at the banner flapping from the Bull and Finch Pub. "Do you know that's supposed to be the bar in the television show *Cheers*?"

He nodded. "That's one landmark I'm familiar with." He placed his hands back into his pockets.

She cocked her head and looked up at him without missing a step. "You do seem the type to know more about bars than nuns." She watched the expression on his face as he laughed. "You should do that more often, it's very becoming." Before he had time to answer, she turned and looked the other direction into the Public Garden. "One of these days, I'm going to have to ride the Swan Boats. Matt says he remembers riding them with your mother once. I guess most children around here get on them sooner or later."

Kevin looked at the boats and then up into the overhanging trees. "She brought us here every summer. Matt may have only come once; he didn't have her very long." Change jingled again and they crossed Arlington Street.

"That's a lovely memory, Kevin. Even though being the eldest strapped you with responsibility, you're lucky to have had your parents as long as you did."

He studied the bricks as they walked. "The last time we came, Matt chased the ducks and nearly fell in. He couldn't have been more than five." He looked at her briefly. "I haven't thought about that in years... such a little kid and look at him now."

"He's going to make a wonderful doctor, Kevin."

"After all the blood, sweat and tears we've shed to get him there, I hope so."

They crossed Berkeley Street and Erin began to laugh.

"Yes?"

"Nothing. I was just thinking about something I did with Matt yesterday." She was quiet for a block, then another laugh escaped. "He's a wreck about starting his OB/GYN rotation. Poor thing, but you can imagine... Without sisters or a mother, I guess the only relationship he's had with women have been romantic ones. Before Nancy and I came along, that is. It's been good for him, if I do say so myself."

"You or romance?"

"Me, of course. I got right up on the dining-room table and let him practice a breast exam. Poor thing turned the color of a radish, but he did just fine, once he got started." Kevin stumbled and Erin thought he'd tripped on a brick, but it was spontaneous laughter that had doubled him over. "Are you all right?" she said, taking his arm.

He nodded.

"Well, anyway, if he weren't so shy, I'd be happy to loan him my breasts anytime. They don't stop traffic, to say the least. Nancy's got a figure to write home about, but she's in England all summer." She looked down at her seersucker bosom, then paused. Kevin was pursing his lips. "I'm sorry,'' she blurted. ''I'm so used to talking about female anatomy. I don't suppose cranberry growers hear this kind of thing much. Breasts are my business, just like bogs are yours.''

''Of course,'' he said, trying not to laugh.

''Anyway, from what Matt tells me, you know your way around the female anatomy just fine.''

He swore under his breath but his blue eyes were bright with amusement. ''You and Matt seem to have quite a relationship. I hope he hasn't given away all my secrets.''

She arched her eyebrows. ''Do you have a lot?''

Kevin changed the subject. ''Are you the farm girl or is that Nancy?''

She took the hint. ''That would be me. It's a dairy farm in the northwest corner of New Jersey, out by the Delaware Water Gap. Lots of lactating cows. My father thinks that's where I get my interest in obstetrics. Who knows?'' She shrugged and put her face up to the breeze. ''I do apologize for my conversation, I'm sure you must think I'm obsessed with my career, or breasts, anyway.'' She watched him astutely avoid glancing at the subject. ''Give me a chiseled set of pectorals, any day.''

They walked the last block. ''And have there been many sets of chiseled pectorals in your life?'' he asked.

Erin searched for an answer. ''Medically, not in my specialty. Socially, a few along the way.''

''Nothing to keep you from your goal?'' Kevin asked.

''Falling in love before I finished school would have been disastrous, or maybe I was just afraid the love of my life would turn out to be from Michigan or Oregon and I'd have to make terrible choices.''

''Too far from home?''

''We're a close family, the way you are. I lost my mother, too, and helped raise my two sisters. I'm comfortable being a day's drive from home. Besides, this is the greatest medical complex in the world. It's what I wanted, a dream I made happen.''

"So here you are, master plan intact," Kevin replied.

"Yes, I guess so."

He grinned at her. "The last virgin on Marlborough Street."

"Well, there was a guy at Princeton."

"Geography's right; fancy credentials."

"I thought so, too. I got myself up there in his suite, necktie on the doorknob..."

"Bells rang and the earth moved, I hope?" Kevin asked.

Erin looked at a flowering quince bush. "Not exactly. He, to put it delicately, was a lot more excited about my mammaries than I was about his pectorals. It was over before it got started."

It wasn't the first time Kevin looked as though he had no idea how to respond and this time it was clearly the choice of subject. He shook his head. If a thirty-seven-year-old face, handsome and etched with character, could register wonder, his came close. "I get the damnedest feeling I should offer condolences or something!"

"I'd say the situation was my fault. Anyway, here we are, three-nineteen! I meant to point out all kinds of historic architectural features on the way."

"Believe me, Erin, this has been an education in itself."

She looked doubtful. "I've been boring and awful."

He pulled a strand of blowing hair from her cheek. "You've been fascinating."

"Thank you," she answered shyly. "I don't get much practice with men other than doctors and technicians. Sorry about all the breast talk."

He took his hand from her hair and dropped his gaze to her breasts before looking at the brickwork behind her. Now that they'd stopped walking, she could see the bleached tips of his thick lashes and a hint of a cleft in his chin. Gray had started at his temples. She liked watching him even though it kept her off balance. Or maybe she enjoyed it *because* it kept her off balance. She was beginning to anticipate the skip in her pulse and the wash of adrenaline; it made her feel alive.

"You were very nice to walk all this way. My father thanks you and your brother thanks you."

"My pleasure."

They smiled at each other spontaneously and the next thing she knew, she'd put her arms up around his neck. She hugged him affectionately, tightly enough so that she felt him pause. His hands were still at his side. "You're just the most wonderful family! I'd be lost in Boston without Matt, and now Sky and Ryan. You're unique, Kevin, every last one of you." She looked around at the Victorian double doors of her building. "You haven't said anything more about my staying at your house while I'm in Millbrook. Truly, I don't want you to feel as though Matt pressured you. There are lots of alternatives."

"Your father will thank me and my brother will thank me."

Erin narrowed her gaze. "Are you teasing me?"

"Yes. Jody'll be happy to hear that you're in town for a week and I'll get a chance to dust off my chaperoning skills."

Erin put her hands on her hips. "I don't need chaperoning, Kevin."

He shook his head slowly. "I was referring to my brother." He put his hands back in his pockets and waited for her to unlock the door, looking as though he'd opened a great, glittering package and hadn't the faintest idea what to do with it.

Three

I'm a boring person," Erin said, as much to herself as to Matt as they carried her luggage to her car.

He smiled. "I don't know, just yesterday you and I had a scintillating conversation about nausea during the second trimester of pregnancy. And what about your thoughts on the immunizing effects of colostrum—I was spellbound after lunch."

She hit him with her briefcase. "Stop teasing, that's exactly what I mean. I'm incapable of discussing anything unless it's related to lactation and childbirth." As if to press the point, she waved *Current Trends in Unmedicated Deliveries* under Matt's nose as they left the building and went into the alley parking area.

"Cheer up. Drew and Holly would love to discuss your specialty and since Sean and Ryan delivered our niece, they're always happy to put their two cents in."

She shook her head at him and unlocked her car door. "It's just that I thought you'd go to Millbrook with me for at least one night."

Matt arched his eyebrows. "So that's it. I'm off to the hospital and you're thrown to the wolves."

"Some nice impersonal motel's what I need." She got into the car and rolled down the window as Matt leaned on the frame.

"No you don't. Kevin will treat you to some home cooking and if things get too boring you can trot up the hill and play with the baby. If I know you, it'll be a week of business and you'll be too busy for anything else, so stop stewing." He patted her shoulder. "I'd love to go, believe me."

"I know." She held up the handwritten directions. "Okay, I'm off. I'll see you next weekend. Knock 'em dead in maternity while I'm gone."

"You knock 'em dead at the clinic, Erin. You'll be wonderful, don't worry."

She wasn't worried about the clinic and she freely admitted as she drove out of the city that she wasn't honestly worried about her one-track conversations. She was worried—anxious, she corrected—about a week of evenings alone with a man who reduced her insides to warm taffy. Anxious and surprised to have found herself reliving their Sunday stroll a thousand times in the two weeks since the luncheon. Anxious in a Christmas Eve, birthday morning, first-day-in-Boston sort of way.

She parted company with the Cape Cod-bound traffic at the Duxbury exit of the highway and from there stole glances at Matt's directions. She wound her way inland from the seacoast, through countryside dotted with picturesque neighborhoods and the suddenly flat acreage of working bogs. The June air through her open windows was sweet and hot, the roads deeply shaded with maples and beech. She slowed down at the first landmark, a golf course and the Millbrook Country Club, smiling at the bordering bogs where Sky had told her she'd run into Ryan after thirteen years. Though she'd never visited, Erin already knew Millbrook through dozens of Branigan anecdotes.

At the bend in the state road she looked for the old BAN-CROFT sign tacked to a tree and put on her blinker. BITTER-SWEET BOGS and BRANIGAN beneath it made her heart jump. She turned onto the rutted lane.

It was as she'd imagined, winding and deeply shaded by a thick stand of pines. The driveway had been impassable during the three-day blizzard that had forced Holly to give birth to Maria Bancroft Branigan at home. It forked at the top of a hill, leaving open vistas in three directions. Drew and Holly's farmhouse lay straight ahead. There was a stroller on the porch and daisies lining the pea gravel.

She turned left, down the hill. The white clapboard Branigan house was rambling, and faced five bog acres and a distant pond. The cozy compound that included Sean and Anne's newer house across the water was hedged in by woodland. Outbuildings dotted the landscape and grass poked through the long strips of sandy soil along dikes and cartpaths where the land was worked.

The driveway formed a courtyard between the house and the gambrel-roofed barn and Erin pulled her car between a pickup truck and a gleaming, cherry-red Corvette. She turned off her ignition and got out as a rhythmic hammering on the barn roof stopped. Half a dozen bodies, stripped to the waist, waved. She shaded her eyes and waved back. There didn't seem to be a woman in sight. In the glare she watched one of them work his way across the strapping to the staging at the side of the building. Once in the shadows, she saw that it was Kevin. Involuntarily she took a deep breath and held it as he worked his way down. He had a ratty bandanna tied around his forehead and a triangle of white zinc oxide on his nose. One hip pocket had been torn from his jeans, leaving a dark blue patch. Sweat glistened on his shoulder blades. He had on workboots and knee pads and a tool belt wrapped his hips as if he were toting six-guns. She had to remind herself to inhale again.

Kevin laughed but stayed a proper distance as he pulled off the bandanna and wiped his neck. "I don't usually greet company in this condition, but welcome to Millbrook. I don't dare get close enough to shake hands."

She waved. "It's great to be here."

"Any trouble finding us?"

She shook her head.

"Good." In spite of his previous statement, he stepped closer. "I'm afraid you're going to be treated like family, Erin. We're putting one last push up there and then we'll quit for the day."

"Could I help?" She watched him glance at her culottes and blouse.

"You stay clean. You could help by making yourself at home. I've put you in the front bedroom. Technically it's still Ryan's, but it's got the best view and a comfortable desk area. I thought you might have some evening paperwork and need a quiet place to yourself. If you'd just let yourself in and make yourself comfortable, I can keep working."

"Of course," she replied, surprised when Kevin began to walk beside her.

"I'll get your luggage, though."

"No need."

"I don't mind."

"You go back to work." They'd reached her car at that point and he raised his finger. "Chivalry, remember?"

"Oh, all right." When he'd pulled her suitcases from the back seat and she'd grabbed her briefcase, Erin looked at the sports car. "Yours?"

Kevin grinned, looking boyish with the addition of the sunscreen on his nose. "My toy. We've had a good couple of years, with the addition of Holly's acreage."

Erin tossed her hair in an unconscious gesture. "If I'd known *that* was sitting in Sky's driveway on Beacon Hill, I'd have insisted on a ride home. I hope a demonstration drive is part of this Millbrook package."

He was quiet, as if the thought hadn't occurred to him. Erin turned and looked directly into his thoughtful gaze. "You told me to feel at home."

"So I did. Well, of course you'll get a ride."

She grinned enthusiastically. "If I help with the shingling, will you let me drive?"

The blue eyes widened.

"Never hurts to ask, Kevin." She blinked innocently and looked hopeful.

"You do jump in with both feet, don't you." He opened the kitchen door and put her luggage in the hallway.

She blew her bangs off her face. "You didn't get where you are today by sitting back, afraid to make your desires known, and neither did I. It might not have occurred to you that I'd like to drive your car so I thought I'd ask." She picked up her suitcases.

Crow's-feet formed as amusement played over his features. He looked at her holding the luggage. "Thanks for letting me know. You're welcome to drive it. I assume you can make it upstairs all right?"

"Absolutely."

"End of the hall, double bed, half a dozen pictures of Sky on the dresser." He turned and left the house, leaving Erin with a powerful aroma of wood chips and manual labor. She leaned against the wall for a full thirty seconds before venturing through the house.

It was clean, airy and masculine, full of fine old furniture and bright rooms. There hadn't been a woman's touch in twenty years and it didn't seem to need one. The second floor held four bedrooms and two baths. In the largest, overlooking the bogs and the woods and the men on the barn roof, Erin found a double bed, a clean desk with a lamp and chair and the snapshots of Sky and Ryan. On the bedspread were a set of towels and empty hangers. She lifted them and looked through the open window in the direction of the rhythmic hammering. She was accepted into this house without question, treated casually, affectionately.

Towels and hangers. Kevin had considered her needs, anticipated her desires for comfort, thought about her even when she wasn't present. The intimacy she felt was out of proportion to the small acts themselves, just as her physical response was. She stood for a long time at the window and watched him work, recognizable at that distance by the white patch on his nose. Under that no-nonsense exterior lurked the endearing qualities of Kevin Branigan. The directors of the Millbrook Medical Clinic weren't the only ones about to benefit from Erin O'Connor's way with people.

She hung her clothes in the space provided in Ryan's closet and changed into cotton slacks, an oversize shirt and cinch belt. She reversed her routine with her hair, piling it into a loose knot at the top of her head since Kevin had never seen it up. Either way added a dramatic touch to her sprite-like appearance. Kevin noticed.

It was nearly four o'clock when Erin arrived in Millbrook and five when she finished unpacking and dressing. Her door was ajar and she opened it to go back downstairs; Kevin was in the hall. They stood assessing one another, then took a step back and smiled. "I didn't hear you," Erin said.

Kevin looked at her hair. "I didn't think you'd still be up here. We'll have to get used to it, I guess," he added, dropping his glance to the stray tendrils along her neck.

"Yes, we will," she replied. He was barefoot, stripped down to his jeans, minus even the bandanna. She glanced at his chest, and, ever the nurse, noted his quick, shallow breaths. He was probably just startled.

"I'm going to shower. Everybody's coming over for a drink." He looked apologetic. "Erin, I'm sorry, I have plans for tonight. I thought Matt would come down with you. Drew and Holly invited you up the hill for dinner, though."

Already a fifth wheel, she thought. "That's not necessary, Kevin, I'll be just fine here alone. I have lots of preparation to take care of."

His smile was slow, as if he were thinking of something else, his eyes still on her hair. "Soothe my guilt, Erin, enjoy an evening up the hill. I don't want you deserted three hours after your arrival."

She agreed finally and he went into his room next to hers. Kevin left without fanfare an hour later. "If you're back before I am, lock up anyway," he'd said, pressing an extra key into her palm. "Keep it for the week so you can come and go as you need to. The dogs can stay out till I get back. I won't be too late." The extended family had gathered in the living room and she watched as he worked his way past Anne and Sean and had a last word with Drew. She heard Holly tell him to say hello to Carol for her and then he was gone. Sky was bent at the window, admiring the Corvette, which gave Erin the excuse to lean over and do the same.

Pea gravel spun from the tires as he drove up the hill. "Impressive pair," Sky said. Erin nodded, keeping her curiosity about Carol to herself.

The evening was delightful. Jody joined her at Drew and Holly's and they talked easily about family and fortune. She was as comfortable in his presence as she was in Matt's. Neither brother had any chemistry for her, though. Jody left early, exhausted from the physical labor of the afternoon. Erin stayed through the ten o'clock feeding and helped put Maria to bed, noting, as Holly lowered the baby into her crib, that she looked none the worse for having been delivered by her uncles in the room downstairs.

Holly laughed. "She doesn't, but I couldn't look Ryan and Sean in the eye for a month. As I'm sure you can see, the Branigans would do anything for each other and heaven help the person who comes between them. I speak from experience!"

"You'd never know it now. They all adore you."

Holly was thoughtful as they went back to the living room. "Kevin said the least and felt the most, I think. When I look back now and see how close I came to selling this right out from under them, I wonder why they didn't just shoot me."

Drew got up from the couch. "Because much as Kevin wanted to, I convinced him it would be more fun my way."

Holly kissed him. "And look where it got you."

Drew smiled. "Kevin should be so lucky."

With the dishes done and the baby asleep, Drew and Holly walked Erin down the hill and waited while she unlocked the door. The dogs, Max and Domino, trotted from the shadows, but stayed on the lawn. She was in bed asleep shortly thereafter.

Erin awoke at one o'clock to the well-tuned hum of Kevin's prize possession and she sat up in bed and watched him park. The courtyard was lighted by floodlights at the corners of the porch and barn and Erin propped her chin on her hand as she watched her host walk through the pool of light and into the darkness. His stride was long and easy, with his hands in his pockets as they'd been along Marlborough Street.

She heard him downstairs as he talked to the dogs, heard the door close, watched the lights go out. The Branigan acreage was plunged into gray moonlight. A bullfrog croaked and peepers sounded through the open window. God was in heaven, and all was right with Kevin's world.

Erin lay in bed, soldier straight, her heart pounding for no reason. "We'll have to get used to this," she repeated, feeling like an eavesdropper as she listened to the man-sounds from the next room.

Bureau drawers opened and closed, wood over wood. A mattress squeaked. He was whistling softly. Whistling didn't seem like a good sign. Then again, he'd come home, hadn't he? His door opened, the bathroom door closed. The intimacy of it was painful and she lay there wondering if he were giving any thought to his guest.

Did he get into bed wondering whether she'd used the towels, whether there'd been enough hangers? Had she gotten home all right? Had the dogs bothered her? The ache in her chest was painful. *Crush* seemed the perfect word for what she was feeling, though she considered herself far too mature to be suffering from one.

She moved under the covers and heard him do the same. If she'd called good-night, he probably would have answered. And if he'd opened her door, she might have given serious thought to welcoming him in.

Four

Erin awoke at seven to bright Millbrook sunshine and she stretched in the Branigan bed, letting the stillness wrap around her. There would be a barn roof full of men soon, she imagined and she got up and dressed quietly.

She gave herself a tour of the kitchen, opening and closing cabinets, taking stock in the pantry. By the time her solitude was broken, she had bacon draining on a paper towel, coffee perked and eggs beaten. Kevin appeared as she was setting the table. He looked appropriately sleepy but freshly shaven and dressed for carpentry.

"I could hardly believe my nose," he said, and used his fingers to brush his hair in place. "Good morning."

Erin smiled, the sight of him lighting her face. "Can't roof on an empty stomach. Matt says you like your eggs scrambled and moist, and your coffee with cream."

He came beside her and poured his own coffee. "Matt tells you a lot about me, I gather."

"You've been his whole life, Kevin. His family is everything to him until he can come up for air." She felt him watching as she stirred the eggs.

"Smells great," he said.

She looked at him. "So do you."

He got his Marlborough Street Look again and cleared his throat. "This is awfully nice of you, but I should be the one at the stove. You're the guest, Erin."

"I prefer *family*, like yesterday. I don't want to disturb your routine any more than I have to. Once I learn my way around the kitchen, I'll be happy to cook for us. My schedule will be lighter than yours, I'm sure."

"I doubt that. Since you have to dress and get out, I'll do breakfast and you can start dinner if I'm still tied up when you get back."

"All right," she replied.

When they were seated and eating he asked about her dinner with his brothers.

"Fun," she answered. "I stayed through Maria's feeding. Jody left to get some rest. He's burning a lot of candles with law *and* the barn. You all seem to run yourselves ragged, don't you."

He shrugged. "Seems to be a Branigan trait."

"I hope you had fun, too, with Carol." She concentrated on her eggs.

"Speaking of running myself ragged?"

"No, speaking of enjoyable evenings. I was just making conversation."

Kevin looked amused. "I always enjoy Carol."

Erin's smile was a little tight. "It was Claudia a while ago."

Kevin leaned back in his chair and palmed his mug. "Yes, it was Claudia a while ago. You have a good memory. Do you do this to my brother?"

"Matt doesn't have a social life at the moment. He gets about as much sleep as you do, for very different reasons."

Kevin was smiling. "Are you keeping track of how much sleep I get?"

Erin put her coffee mug to her lips and kept it there, long after she'd taken the last swallow. "Your car woke me, and you were whistling."

"Was I?" Two legs of the chair left the floor as he leaned farther. "I'll try to remember not to."

"Then you'll be going out tonight?"

"Hadn't planned to." He closed his eyes and she could see the curl in his sunlightened lashes. Kevin came forward slowly and when the chair was back on four legs, he got up, plate and mug in hand. "Delicious breakfast. Thanks. Matt does know what I like, I guess."

"I've paid attention," Erin replied.

Kevin looked at her from the sink, still amused. "Yes, I can see that." He slapped his thigh for Max and Domino and the Labrador retrievers followed him through the door to the porch. He left it open and through the screen Erin caught glimpses of him pulling on his workboots and strapping on the tool belt. Ryan's Bronco pulled in next to the Corvette and she heard him call to Drew, who was coming down the hill.

Kevin clomped back in and let the screen door slam. "Almost forgot the zinc oxide. I don't mean to leave you with the dishes, Erin. They can wait."

"I don't mind," she said. "You go work."

"In a minute." He managed to work around her until she stepped aside and let him rinse the cast-iron skillet. "You didn't come down here to wait on me or clean up after me. Or be kept awake by my whistling." He grinned when she looked uncomfortable. "It's been a long time since anyone waited up for me, Erin." He was back out the door before she could think of a wisecrack.

The woods bordering the bogs were cool and Erin spent the better part of the morning walking the paths, looking for Indian pipes in the carpet of pine needles, and listening to the whistle as the breeze caught the evergreens. Anne and her daughters were sunning on the edge of the pond and she called Erin to come for a swim later.

She returned to the house by way of the dike and shaded her eyes to look first at the distant laundry strung between the trees behind Holly's kitchen, then at the roof of the barn. She arrived at the courtyard as Kevin jumped from the staging.

"Could I get you guys some lunch?" she asked.

"They'll fend for themselves," he replied, pulling a discarded shirt over his chest. "I've got to run to the lumberyard, we've been waiting for it to open."

"Where's the lumberyard?" She was growing quite fond of the way he looked in nothing but ancient denim.

"Off the common, behind the police station." He began to walk toward the vehicles in the courtyard.

Erin slipped her arm through Kevin's which took more courage than she hoped was evident. She expected The Look and she got it. "Wonderful. I've heard so much about the police station and Sky's house. You'll let me tag along, won't you?"

"I don't have time for a tour, Erin. Maybe tonight." He was warm where their shoulders and arms pressed each other, but she dropped her grasp and moved a discreet distance. "You might as well come along, though," he added.

She took his arm back. "I don't suppose we could fit the lumber into your juicy little sports car?"

He laughed. "You're a persistent little thing! Sorry, the truck'll have to do."

She shrugged. "We'll save the Corvette for the real tour." She liked the way he looked when he was at a loss for words.

They drove into Millbrook in the BRANIGAN CRANBER-RIES late-model pickup truck. "The view's better from this height, anyway," she said, as the countryside gave way to civilization. A wide strip of park bordered in spring flowers and blossoming shrubs separated the two sides of Main Street. Kevin pointed out Sean's truck at the firehouse, drove slowly past the boutiques, deli, post office and white steepled churches, letting Erin take a good long look. "It's darling, if you can say that about a town," she sighed. "Which is Schuyler House?"

Kevin pointed across the street at the line of stately colonials and Victorians lining the common. She leaned next to him and peered through his window. As hard as he'd been working, there was still a hint of after-shave.

"Sky's is the white brick-ender with the lilac hedge and iron fence."

"Beautiful," she murmured. "I suppose they'll live here permanently after the wedding?"

"Absolutely. Sky's determined to keep Schuyler House in the family, which is what brought her back to Millbrook in the first place."

"The wedding'll be here, too, she says."

Kevin nodded and then began to laugh. Erin watched him until it became obvious that he wasn't about to share the joke. "Well?"

"Nothing."

"That's a lot of ha-ha-ha over nothing."

"It's nothing, really, just a private joke about their honeymoon."

"Too much for my almost-virgin ears? Come on, Kevin, I told you what was making me laugh when we walked home, about Matt's breast—"

"I *know* you told me about the exam." His cheeks darkened and the flush colored the area not already whitened by the sunscreen. "They've been saying they're going to honeymoon on the Millbrook Country Club golf course."

Erin waited, Kevin sighed. "That's not the punch line," she said.

"No, it's not. The golf course is where they lost their virginity when they were sweethearts."

"And then the Schuylers shipped Sky off to Europe and college and Ryan joined the army and they didn't see each other for thirteen years. I know all about it. I think it's the most painfully romantic story I ever heard," Erin added.

"You would, wide-eyed innocent that you are."

"I'm not!"

Kevin patted her knee. "Relax, I meant it as a compliment." He put the truck back into gear and continued the drive. "You knew all about it. Is there anything you don't know about us?"

Erin turned sideways in her seat and looked at his handsome profile. "Why don't you tell me some of your deep, dark secrets and I'll tell you whether I already knew about them."

"Erin..."

She patted *his* knee as they turned onto Pilgrim Street and passed the police station. "Ryan's old headquarters," she said.

"Yes."

"So Ryan chased rich girls around golf courses and Drew convinced the girl next door not to sell out. Sean's been in love since puberty. What about Kevin? Did you ever smoke behind the barn and sow wild oats and all that other boy-becomes-a-man stuff, or were you too busy playing role model?'' She kept looking at him, studying the discomfort and the sunburn and the tilt of his chin. ''Are you thinking of a nice way to ask me to mind my own business?''

''Yes.'' He kept his eyes on the road and swung the truck through the gates of the lumberyard.

''Wide-eyed innocents can get away with being nosy.''

He turned off the ignition and looked at her. ''They should also be careful that their feelings don't get trampled in the process.''

It was meant to end the conversation and Kevin opened his door. Erin took a deep breath. ''Would you trample on mine?''

He studied her hair and then slid from the seat. ''Never intentionally.''

Kevin returned to the bogs with lumber in the back, hinges and a paper sack of roofing nails. Erin returned with a growing sense of excitement, a deepening sense of challenge. She was drawn to his personality and disturbed by his physical presence. It was delicious. She was fascinated by what he offered, curious by what he held back and just confident enough to keep pressing.

Whether by necessity or design, Erin wasn't alone again with him for the rest of the day. The afternoon was crammed with hard work and Kevin managed to stay forty feet above her until midafternoon. Sky was the last to arrive, with a case of soda in the trunk of her ancient Mercedes. Kevin called a break and Sky made them promise not to touch anything stronger than cola until they were done for the day. She then gave Kevin an aristocratic smile. ''This is a bribe, handsome. Ryan's boys from the Police League are at my house.''

Kevin's face clouded immediately and he looked at Ryan. ''You promised me the weekend!''

His brother touched his shoulder. "They're going to do Sky's carriage house. They only need me to help with the staging. I'll be back, I swear! The paint's there, the brushes..."

"Go then," Kevin muttered. It was a side of him Erin had only glimpsed New Year's Eve when Ryan was making similar promises. To Erin's surprise, Sky leaned over and gave Kevin a resounding kiss.

"Could be worse, future brother-in-law. He could be off in his squad car with a .357 magnum strapped to his hip, working the midnight-to-eight shift. He gave it up for you," she added, barely above a whisper. To Erin she called, "See you at the clinic in the morning," and then she and Ryan drove their cars back to Schuyler House.

"Lives of their own," Erin said to Kevin as he watched the dust settle. "It's what you've wanted for each of them."

"So it is," he replied before he left her for the roof.

Without asking, Erin took on the job of loading debris into the back of the cranberry truck used for hauling. It was already piled with shreds of tar paper and shingles. She set about throwing in loose scraps that littered the yard. Within the hour she'd tied her blouse up in a knot under her breasts, as close as she'd get to stripping as the men had. She redid her hair, pulling it tightly up away from her neck. She handled the scraps with gardening gloves and stopped only when the phone rang.

"Erin?" Kevin shouted from above.

"Got it," she called and followed the ring to the storage room in the barn. "Branigan Cranberries," she said into the receiver.

"Holly, it's Carol. I know the boys are working, just tell Kevin I called to thank him for last night. He sure knows how to show a girl a good time. I can hear the hammering, I'll let you go. Tell him for me, will you?"

"Yes, yes I will."

The receiver clicked before she could correct the mistake. Erin went back out in the sun and put her arm over her eyes as Drew, Kevin and Jody peered down at her. Drew gave her a wolf whistle and she swished her hips. "Just trying to keep up with you guys," she called. "The phone was for you, Kevin. Carol said to tell you that you sure know how to show a girl a good time."

She watched as he shook his head and laughed at whatever Jody's low remark had been. They talked among themselves, out of earshot and she lowered her arm slowly, feeling foolish. When the day's debris was in the back of the truck, she left the men to their hammering and walked back over the dike to the pond. Anne and her daughters were back, settled on a sandy area obviously used for family activities. They all waved as Erin approached. "Where's your suit, it must be eighty degrees!" Anne called.

Erin shook her head. "I never thought to pack one. I'll just dunk my feet. I really came over to take a breather from all the noise."

Anne laughed. "All the noise and all the masculinity. I suppose they're up there swearing and spitting and scratching as always." She turned to her toddlers. "Girls, come and meet Uncle Matt's friend from Boston, Erin O'Connor." They shook hands dutifully.

Anne put her hand on the oldest. "Suzanne Gates Branigan and this is Kathleen Ryan Branigan, known as Kate."

"How do you do," Erin said solemnly to both of them. "Ryan must be a family name."

"Kathleen Ryan was my mother-in-law's maiden name," Anne replied.

"Did you know her?"

"Everybody knew Kate Branigan and her six boys. I'm a townie, too. Sean, Drew and I shared one class or another from kindergarten up. The three of us were sixteen when their parents were killed in the car accident. It was terrible, of course. Drew and Ryan were just awful for a while. Poor Kevin had to answer for most of their carrying on.

"There was talk of splitting them up among relatives, none of whom are in Millbrook. Kevin wouldn't hear of it. Peter was up on the hill with his own bogs and just as much determination. He convinced the state and the schools that things would work out, and became their legal guardian. Kevin took it on himself to save the entire Branigan family reputation while Peter Bancroft kept the business going. Kevin was two years ahead of us in school and he came back and chaperoned our senior prom like he was thirty. That man has commanded respect since he was eighteen. The Chamber of Commerce has awarded him twice, it was his idea for the company to underwrite an annual concert of the Plymouth Philharmonic. If ever there were a phoenix rising from the ashes, it's Number One Son rambling around in that big old farmhouse over there across the bogs."

"He doesn't seem to mind the solitude."

Anne smiled. "He's due for some, wouldn't you say?" She got up from the sand to settle an argument between the children and came back as Erin was splashing herself with the water. "Would you consider borrowing one of my suits? We're about the same size. I've got a size eight suit, clean and dry right in the laundry room. You look as though you could use a swim."

Erin relaxed. "If you really wouldn't mind."

"I really wouldn't. I can't leave the kids, but please feel free to get it yourself. There's a powder room right off the kitchen."

The suit was a blue maillot that complimented Erin's coppery hair as well as Anne's carrot-colored curls. It fit perfectly with the exception of the bra top, in which Erin was lost. She shrugged and went back to the pond. The New England water was cool, wonderfully refreshing and she let her hair float on the surface around her as she skimmed the surface in a crawl.

Her concentration was broken by shrieks around her and the thundering steps of four men racing each other over the dike. Erin stayed in the water and watched in amazement. Ryan had returned and seemed to have won the race, although it was hard to tell as the four of them hopped from one leg to another, yanking off boots, socks, belts and wallets. They shouted insults and challenges as the paraphernalia hit the sand. They plunged, one after the other in a tangled mass, into the water like a pack of schoolboys let loose for the summer. Erin got out as unobtrusively as possible.

"Was I just talking about maturity?" Anne asked as Erin sat down.

Erin shook her head. "There is a certain puppylike quality."

"They play as hard as they work. What on earth are you doing?" Anne blurted as Erin broke her concentration.

"Fixing your bathing suit so you can't look down at my navel," she replied as she grabbed and shook a pair of navy tube socks and stuffed them into the bra cups. The navy cotton forced her breasts to rise in hefty swells above the bodice. Erin adjusted them and gave herself a satisfied shimmy as a shadow passed over her heretofore unexposed flesh. She craned her neck and blinked at the figure towering—and dripping—over her. She put one hand behind her head and licked her lips. "How do you like me so far?"

Kevin knelt, cleared his throat and shook his head. Erin followed his gaze to her bosom. There was a blue cotton heel peeking from the left cup. "Miss O'Connor, that wouldn't be my sock?"

She shrugged and stuffed it back in. "Nature's not always perfect."

Five

After the turmoil and shenanigans, the property settled into a summer stillness. Erin left the pond and had showered and changed by the time the brothers disbanded. She puttered in the kitchen while Kevin went upstairs.

"You're spoiling me," he said, when he returned and found dinner ready and the table set.

"It's about time somebody did," Erin replied.

They ate at dusk with long silences punctuated by conversation. Kevin was as quiet as Erin was vivacious and she reminded herself that it was Kevin's rhythm that ran the house. She was growing comfortable with it.

"Tired?" he asked.

"A little. It's a nice tired though."

"You were a big help this afternoon, I meant to tell you." He winced as he picked up their plates.

"Blisters?"

"Splinters. I got a handful when I gave my gloves to Jody." He insisted on dish detail while Erin fed the dogs, noticing, while they ate, the way Kevin continued to favor his right hand. Without asking she went upstairs and rummaged through the medicine cabinets until she found tweezers, Band-Aids and an ointment. She also brushed her hair and freshened her lipstick.

She found Kevin in the family room off the kitchen, reading a *Wall Street Journal*. He looked up and frowned. "What are you up to?"

Erin grinned and waved the tweezers. "House call. Won't hurt much."

"Thanks, but I can take care of it."

"You're risking infection and judging from the way you've been favoring it, you'll risk sloppiness or injury tomorrow if we don't take care of it now. It's your right hand and I can get them out a lot less painfully than you can fumbling around with your left."

Kevin leaned back in his chair and studied her. "How'd you get so bossy?"

"Same way you did, early responsibility. It's also my line of work, although most of my patients don't talk back since they're in labor." She sat on the couch next to him and looked at the portrait on the wall of Kathleen Branigan and six children. The room was full of mementos, book-lined shelves, small, framed photographs. Kevin was silent until she brought her attention back to the task at hand.

There was a floor lamp between them that she pulled over as she set the supplies on the coffee table. She opened her palm in a silent request until he reluctantly opened his hand over hers. It felt wonderful. "You should have taken these out sooner," she said with an attempt at professionalism. "These are quite deep, did you lose your balance?"

"Ow!"

Erin looked up at him and her hair tumbled into her face from its tenuous loop around her ear. "Kevin, did you nearly fall off the roof and grind your hand into the cedar shingle?"

"Once."

She made a tsk-tsk noise. "I'd think you'd be more careful, especially since you broke your leg in that awful fall last year."

"Year before last. You've heard that story, too?"

She got back to work. "Yes. Poor Holly had to come over here and play nurse and there were dozens of you, not just one cantankerous bachelor."

"*Poor* Holly was the cause of the accident and only three of us were living here full time, Drew, Ryan and me. Ow, damn it." This time he pulled his hand away.

She yanked it back. "Behave yourself. I suppose you think you're intimidating." She blew at her bangs.

"But I do intimidate you, don't I?" As he asked, he took his free hand and lightly pushed her hair back behind her ear.

If she kept her head down she hoped he might not see the color across her cheeks. "A little, sometimes." She moved to his thumb.

"You love nursing, don't you?" he said when she didn't look up.

"As much as you love your work. It's second nature to me, though I haven't had much practice using my administrative skills. All that will change tomorrow."

"But caring for people is your first love?"

"My mother died when I was seventeen. She was ill for quite some time and I was fortunate enough to have been allowed to help. I suppose an analyst would say my career stems from the lactating cows and that experience. Who knows why we're the way we are?" Kevin's hand was no longer tense and when she finished with his thumb, she opened his palm again, this time against her thigh. Gently she eased a sliver from under his nail. "I like to think I make a difference." She glanced up at his face to see if he was grimacing, but his eyes were closed. Butterflies rose in her stomach.

"The hardest part about losing my mother was facing my own anger and my guilt about feeling angry. I had a chance to say goodbye, though, and that helped." Unconsciously she lowered her voice and looked at the portrait behind him. "You have your mother's smile. It must have been tougher for you, losing both of them so suddenly. You must have been furious underneath, being strapped with all the responsibility." She let go of his hand finally and placed the tweezers in an ashtray, then picked up the ointment and Band-Aids.

Kevin took them from her. "I didn't have any right to be angry and I didn't have the time to dwell on it." He dabbed each of the wounds and waved his hand, avoiding her glance. "Let's have some coffee," he said abruptly.

Erin refused to take the hint. "Kevin, you must have been. Your parents' death yanked your future right out from under you, forcing you to be a man when you should have stayed a kid. Anger's a natural part of grieving, how else were you expected to get on with your life?"

He stood up and the dogs raised their heads. "It was a long time ago, Erin." He glanced at the portrait and then slapped his thigh. As Max and Domino trotted to the screen door, Erin looked at Kevin expectantly. His blue eyes were dark, his expression guarded. "Thanks for the first aid. It's time for their run." He snapped on the outside lights and pushed open the screen door before he turned back and looked at her. "I'll be out for a while."

"Want some company?"

He shook his head. "Another time, Erin. Good night."

He was gone before she had a chance to collect her wits, gone from his own house. Through the open window, Erin heard him call the dogs and she went into the kitchen and looked out into the warm June night. Kevin was crossing through the lamplight at the edge of the barn and she watched his shadowed figure as he stopped and leaned against the truck. He put his good hand up to his forehead and guilt stabbed her. She'd probed where she had no right, until the man who'd told her he'd never intentionally trample her feelings had left.

She could barely swallow as she went back into the family room for the supplies and carried them with her upstairs. She busied herself with preparing for Monday morning and went to bed.

Erin awoke to bright sun and anxiety. Her excitement for the professional challenge that lay ahead was tempered with caution. She rolled over and looked around the room. Her medical papers were on the desk, her clothes in the closet. In this rambling house she knew where to find tweezers and laundry detergent, dog food and roofing nails. Her dusty sneakers were on the porch next to well-worn workboots and her windbreaker hung on the peg next to foul-weather slickers as if it belonged there. She had jumped into Kevin Branigan's life with both feet and stuffed her bathing suit with his socks. Was nothing sacred, she asked herself. His hospitality wasn't an invitation to invade his privacy.

She berated herself as she dressed and wound her hair into a chignon at the nape of her neck. When she'd added makeup and smoothed her dress she picked up her briefcase and opened the door. Kevin was across the hall with one foot poised on the threshold of the bathroom. He wore pajama bottoms and a night's growth of beard. He swore and closed his eyes. "I thought you were still asleep. I'm embarrassed."

"Too nervous," she blurted. "Up early."

His blue eyes were clear and bright as he looked at her. "You don't look nervous," he said.

"You don't look embarrassed," she replied. You look gorgeous, she added to herself.

"I was supposed to make you breakfast, can you wait?"

"Don't worry, I couldn't swallow more than toast, anyway," Erin answered. She took a deep breath as he moved into the bathroom. "Kevin, I'm sorry."

"About your appetite?"

"About last night. I didn't mean to trample all over your feelings, it's none of my business. I talk too much and I was out of line. It won't happen again."

Kevin crossed his arms over his chest and leaned into the door. "Yes, I suspect it will. Don't look hurt, Erin, it's part of your personality, all fresh and curious and well-meaning. It can be unnerving, but I'm sure it's part of what makes you a good nurse."

"You have every right to your privacy, Kevin."

He smiled. "Apparently not this week."

"Are you trying to cheer me up?" she murmured.

"I hurt you, Erin, I didn't mean to. You didn't trample, it was more like a tap dance. I did the trampling, I'm sorry."

She smiled back. "So am I." They said their goodbyes in the hall and the tension eased out of her. Halfway down the stairs she had a thought and went back to the bathroom. Kevin was leaning over the sink, his jaw wrapped in shaving cream. He was pulling the razor along his cheek.

"Kevin, I owe you for this one. Tomorrow you can put on a business suit and I'll stand at the vanity in my nightgown just to even things up." He made a choking sound and nicked his jaw as she drew the door closed behind her and went down to the kitchen. He had the most expressive eyebrows she'd ever seen.

The Millbrook Medical Clinic was on the Duxbury Road. Erin smiled as she drove past the country club's golf course and imagined Sky and Ryan eluding the ever-vigilant, Big Brother Kevin. Back then he would have been about the age she was now and she would have been about six. Six! It seemed impossible that so many years separated them.

She parked the car next to Sky's Mercedes and took a deep breath, bringing her thoughts back to the matters at hand. Men and women were anxiously awaiting her expertise. Erin entered the building determined to give them their money's worth. She spent the morning with the board of directors, a mix of medical and business professionals, who outlined what she'd already read in their grant proposals. Their concerns, and Erin's involvement were focused on OB/GYN services. Federal start-up money had been matched by state funding and private donations, enough to provide a salary for an executive director and a staff of four.

Her associates for the week were Marnie Taylor, financial director for the entire clinic, and Winifred Montgomery, an obstetrician affiliated with Plymouth General Hospital. "As you know," Dr. Montgomery said over ham sandwiches in the boardroom, "demographics support the need for childbirth preparation classes in Millbrook. The hospital's a forty-minute drive for anyone this far east of Plymouth and by offering them here, we'll serve a group who wouldn't have used them otherwise. Beginning the first of July, we'll offer weekly sessions for patients scheduled to deliver at P.G.H., with the last class at the hospital so they can tour the maternity floor and delivery rooms. I've got you penciled in with the instructors for this afternoon and tomorrow morning."

Marnie slid a typed sheet across the table. "The seed money's provided enough for visual aids, including the two films you use in Boston and the booklets and handouts on prenatal nutrition. If you'll review them, I'll put the order in tomorrow."

Erin nodded and looked over the list. By the end of the day, she'd established her priorities and finished half the instruction for the class. The hired instructors were seasoned professionals, both R.N.'s, as she was. Erin used a vacant office for her temporary headquarters and it wasn't until four o'clock that she sat down at the word processor to put her thoughts on paper. At five, Sky stuck her head in.

"How's your first day been?"

Erin pushed her chair back and smiled. "Frantic, but productive. How about lunch tomorrow?"

"Sounds good. Don't stay too long. I'm off to feed my hungry roofer and check on the progress in my bedrooms. Things okay with Kevin?"

Erin nodded. "Has he said something to Ryan? I think I'm a little overpowering. I'm trying not to be too disruptive but I tend to pester him. I'm sure he's relieved to have me here all day."

"You would have been welcome with me if the rooms were ready. Next time around, come to Schuyler House. Don't worry about Kevin, it's just his nature. He and Ryan were always the quiet ones. That house is big enough for both of you and if he gives you any trouble, just tell him I said so. One last thing, my mother has sent out invitations to a formal engagement party, last part of July. You'll get yours when you get back to Marlborough Street."

Erin rubbed the muscles in her shoulder. "Thanks for including me. See you in the morning." When Sky had left, Erin turned back to her report and lost herself in the analysis. When she finished and glanced at her watch it was nearly seven.

Kevin's farmer's porch smelled of barbecued chicken and as the dogs barked and came to greet her, her host pushed open the screen door. His workboots had been exchanged for loafers and his hair was damp from a recent shower. The sight of him did more for her than a shot of caffeine. She wished she'd put on lipstick before she'd left the clinic. He held the door and she went into the family room with her blazer on her arm and the briefcase in her hand, both of which she dropped into the nearest chair.

"Hard day at the office?" Kevin said.

Erin let the pleasure of looking at him dance over her. He was the only man she'd seen since the board meeting and the only one she cared to. She smiled at the small Band-Aid on his chin. "Yes," she finally said, "hard, but challenging."

"Why don't you tell me about it over some wine while I get dinner?"

Her brown eyes widened. "Kevin, you should have eaten, you must be starving after working all day! Please don't let me disrupt your routine this week," she added as she followed him into the kitchen.

He poured her a drink. "I think we'd better face the fact that you have, kiddo, and get on with it. Dinner's on hold, ready any time you are. Go on upstairs and get comfortable, then we'll sit down. You can tell me all about what you're doing for the women of the community and I'll tell you about grading the access roads at the bogs."

She narrowed her gaze. "You're teasing."

"Yes, I suppose I am, but I'll listen if you will."

Erin went up and changed and let her hair down even though the temperature was still high. Over wine and chicken they talked business. Safe subjects, but good conversation, which renewed Erin's spirits the way Kevin's presence did. She was relaxed and animated. The constant stimulation of Kevin's closeness and the challenge presented by his reserve made her heart sing. They did the dishes side by side while she got a lesson in bog productivity. Kevin talked far more easily about the Land Assessment Act and taxes on their holdings than he did about his personal life. Erin listened intently to his theories on owning heavy equipment versus renting it when needed. At least he was talking.

Her feet and legs were bare and she caught him glancing at them as he put leftovers into the refrigerator. It seemed encouraging, like preliminary games to what she began to hope might lie ahead.

"I suppose you do a fair amount of the administrative work for all of this. Do you like it as well as the physical part?" Erin asked.

He closed the fridge. "Holly's taken over a lot of the business end; she's got more of a head for figures. Paperwork can be a nice change, though. And you? Isn't this your first opportunity at administration, putting all that master's degree knowledge to work?"

She frowned. "You know I have my master's in public health?"

Kevin's smile was slow. "Matt probably talks as much about you as he's talked about me."

They faced each other at opposite counters, reading each other's expressions. "Kevin, you do know that there's nothing between me and your brother, don't you? Matt's a wonderful friend, nothing more."

"There should be. You'd be perfect for him."

"We don't love each other in that way, Kevin. There's no chemistry, no tension in the air—you know what I'm trying to say." She sipped the last of her wine and looked directly into his eyes. "Matt and I have never had to fight that magical, physical pull, the kind that blows a New Year's kiss all out of proportion and makes every sentence full of innuendo. You know the feelings I'm talking about.''

"Do I?" he asked, his eyes still on hers.

"I think so."

The sun had set and the lights were on. Through the window she could see the distant glow from Sean and Anne's. Neither of them spoke until she turned back from the window. "Do you mind if I watch the ball game?" Kevin finally asked.

"Please do whatever you usually do. I'll be at my desk for a while before I go to bed. Don't feel as though you have to entertain me, Kevin." *Don't feel the constant need to retreat,* she pleaded silently. "If you usually date, I'll be fine here alone. I don't want Carol to think ... anything." Even saying her name hurt a little.

Kevin folded their napkins and poured himself a cup of coffee. She heard him sigh. "Erin?"

"Go watch the game; I'll be going upstairs in a minute."

"I will. There's been some unintentional trampling."

"I know and I'm sorry, I said so this morning."

"On my part," he interrupted.

Erin looked at him and waited. "Carol Fraser is our accountant. She's been Branigan Cranberries's C.P.A. since the sixties. She's beautiful, happily married and pushing fifty. Every June we renew the professional relationship with a handshake and a steak dinner, a tradition my father started and Peter continued until he died. I've taken over these past few years."

Erin tried to hide her obvious relief, but the look on Kevin's face told her it had been a pitiful attempt. "You wanted me to think there was more to the relationship?"

"Yes," he murmured uncomfortably. "It was unintentional, but when I realized what conclusions you were jumping to, I thought it was a good idea to let it ride." He raked his hair with his fingers. "It put distance between us."

She inhaled sharply. "And if I thought you were seriously seeing someone else, I might not make quite such a fool of myself, the way I did a minute ago. It didn't help, did it? I just kept plowing along until you had to come right out and lay it on the line." He put his hand out to her but she stepped sideways.

"Erin, of course I know there's something between us, but it can't get in the way. You're new at this and I've been around the block a few times. Can you trust me when I tell you to wait? Someone like Matt, like Jody—"

She cut him off with a curt, "Please, Kevin, you've said enough." There was little she could do about the hurt in her eyes and less about the flush that burned her cheeks. Instead, she slapped her thigh and pushed open the screen door as Max and Domino trotted eagerly from the family room. "I'm walking the dogs and if you were any kind of gentleman, you'd just glue yourself to that television set or go up to bed." The door slapped against its frame as she and the dogs went out into the June night air.

Six

Erin kept right on going, across the lawn, across the courtyard, between the Corvette and the pickup truck, until she was out in the shadows. She threw a stick for Max and Domino and kicked the sand under her feet. "You're both male, too," she muttered.

Without shoes she had to walk gingerly over the cartpath and as the breeze blew back her hair she prayed it would cool her complexion. Here in his own world, Kevin Branigan was stuck with a starry-eyed neophyte. So starry-eyed and obvious, he'd felt compelled to trump up a romance to keep her at bay. Her blush deepened as she thought about her two days of perky, irreverent flirting. She should have told him she never would have gone so far if she hadn't sensed the same feelings in him. "Been around the block a few times." Didn't that imply acting on those kinds of emotions without regret?

Under the rising moon she walked to the end of the bogs and turned back, concentrating as she went on the distant croak of a bullfrog and the panting of the dogs. She crossed the lawn and skirted the compost pile and neat vegetable garden, looking at the dark bundles of roofing shingles. At the edge of the barn she put her hand out and touched the staging but kept walking. Ahead of her there was movement in the pool of light from the rafters. Kevin was leaning against his truck.

"Hi," he said softly.

"Aren't you afraid I might get too close out here in the dark, romantic moonlight?"

"Erin, please. After a thousand apologies for disturbing my routine, you take *my* dogs, run them over *my* bogs and send me to *my* room. I'm trying to behave like a gentleman, that's what's gotten me into this mess. I've embarrassed you and I'm sorry." He watched her run her big toe through the grass. "I'm going to work out here in the shop for a while. The house is yours."

"I don't need all of it."

"Even when you're not here to turn my life upside down, Erin, I'm likely to be found working in the barn. Peter found me here after the accident."

Erin looked at his face, half shadowed, as he stared into the barn's cavernous opening. "Kevin, you don't have to tell me any more. We'll just wind up apologizing again."

"You asked me if I got angry."

"It was none of my business," she whispered. The air smelled of honeysuckle and cedar as she looked at him.

"I broke every window in the back of the barn. I was on the baseball team that spring, had been all through school. It was my father's love; he coached me and the others by the hour out here. We were heading for the championships, a winning season, but he died right in the middle. I was fine for weeks, just kept playing and pushing and winning. Millbrook won the division title. Peter went with me to the banquet and that night he told me that he and I would see that nobody split up the kids; the two of us would keep everything the way it was." Kevin closed his eyes and put his head back against the truck window as he sighed.

"My grandmother was in the house with us, Peter still lived up the hill. I came out here to swing the bat in the dark and something just snapped. Jamie Branigan, who'd put all those years into my baseball playing, had missed it all. He died before I won. It's crazy, I know, but I couldn't believe they'd left me before the end of the season, Jamie and Kate, the team's biggest boosters. That night I picked up the bat and started to swing...just kept on swinging until every window was out. Gram was asleep but Peter heard me. He came down the hill and I thought he'd beat the life out of me." Kevin stopped and pressed a fist to his brow. Erin touched his shoulder.

"He didn't even get angry," Kevin continued. "He took me in there and helped me clean it up. Told me I had no choice but to get on with my life and that I couldn't do anything for my brothers until I faced up to my own feelings."

"Harsh words," Erin whispered.

"The truth. 'They didn't mean to leave you, but they did and you've got every right to be angry.' Peter said it then and you said it last night, Erin. I don't know that I'm any better at facing my feelings now than I was then. Peter Bancroft bought us Max and got all of us through the first year. He was a great man."

"Thank you for sharing, Kevin," Erin added.

"It's about time I did. It's been chewing at me all day."

"Because I dredged it all up last night."

Kevin turned and smiled at her. "I think we've had enough apologies for one night. Take the dogs home, I'll see you in the morning."

She would have given anything at that moment if he'd bent and kissed her, but Kevin looked as though he'd shared too much already. She called the dogs and began to race them as he went into the barn. Fifty feet into the running, Erin cried out and dropped to the grass, a searing pain racing from the arch of her foot. Kevin reached her as she drew her knee to her chest.

"Your ankle?" he asked as he knelt next to her.

She bit her lip and shook her head as he pulled her into the light. "The bottom of my foot," she gasped.

"Let me have a look." He tried to hold her foot but she pushed against him until his grip immobilized her.

"I can do it," she groaned, digging her fingers into his arm. "Please, Kevin...that hurts...a lot!" Tears stung her eyes as she pressed her face into his shoulder.

"So does your grip on my arm," he replied. "Hold still. I had to, while you dug splinters out of me."

"Ow!"

"There," he said angrily, twirling a roofing nail between his thumb and fingers. "Erin, you should know better than to come out here with bare feet. You're not stupid." He stopped and pulled her to him when he saw the trail of tears over her cheeks. "Forgive me, I'm the one that embarrassed you until you left the house. Next time don't leave in such a hurry."

The lump in her throat made it impossible to answer with more than a nod as she held her head to his chest, his hand in her hair. Under her ear she could hear the thumping of his heart from the scare she'd given him. Ever the protector, she thought. Gently, he pushed back up and brushed her cheeks with his fingers.

"I'd better get inside and take a look at this," she managed, hobbling onto one foot only to be swept into his arms. "Kevin, you can put me down, I'm just fine."

"Stop being so bossy. Men are supposed to do things like this."

"I thought you wanted distance between us. First I get confessions and now Rhett Butler. If I weren't mistaken, I'd say you didn't know what you want."

He started toward the house. "What I want and what I intend to do about it are two very different things. That's not Tara over there." He might have continued but the walk jostled her and she whimpered. "Hold on," he murmured suddenly serious, nuzzling her face with his head.

Erin took him literally, locked her hands around his neck and burrowed back against his shoulder. She smiled in the dark and let the physical sensations—none of which resembled pain—seep into her. She fit into Kevin Branigan's arms like warm chocolate into a candy mold. She breathed in short sighs against the back of his ear and as he worked his foot into the screen door frame and eased it open, he moved his head away from hers. "Here we are," he whispered.

He lowered her into the straight-back chair at the kitchen table and went into the pantry for a paper towel. Through the door, Erin caught sight of him pressing his arms against the lid of the washing machine, looking for all the world as if he were fighting for composure. When he came back to her, he dabbed the wound. "Not much blood."

Erin nodded. "Puncture. I just need to clean it and soak it so it will heal from the inside out. I'd better get up to the bathtub, my foot's filthy."

Kevin looked at his watch. "Should I drive you to the emergency room for a tetanus shot?"

"No, my inoculations are up to date, a little first aid should do it." She touched a bloodstain on his thigh. "I've ruined your khakis, I'm sorry."

Kevin put his hand over hers and lifted it. "No harm done. Let's get this taken care of." With that he scooped her again into his arms and started for the staircase.

"Why, Rhett, darlin', what do you have in mind?"

Kevin made a scoffing noise. "What I have in mind is not getting blood on my carpet. Keep your foot up."

"I'm beginning to understand why you've been a bachelor all these years."

At the second-floor landing she wiggled from his grasp and hobbled to the edge of the tub where she sat, fully clothed in her shorts and shirt, and soaked her injury. Kevin laid out the antibiotic cream and bandages, then puttered in his room until she'd finished. As she limped from the bathroom he met her in the hall.

"How's it feel?"

"Much better, thanks. Since it's right in the middle of my instep, it doesn't hurt to walk, carefully that is. It should heal fine in a day or so. Thanks for bringing me in. I was careless, you were right." They looked at each other and she smiled. "Thank you for talking to me as much as you did. It answers a lot of questions about the man you are."

"Don't dwell on the man I am, Erin. I'm quiet by nature. I'm settled into this life, it's been a long time coming."

"The solitude?"

"Solitude, financial security, independence. I've taken care of a lot of people for a long time. I needed to let go as much as they did. Drew and Ryan's settling down is good for all of us." He had been looking at her hair and he absentmindedly brushed a tangle of it with his knuckles, then held it in his hand. "Wonderful color," he said almost to himself.

Erin held her breath and stepped up against him. Kevin put his arms around her, one across her back, one still in her hair, pulling her to him. His heart hammered against her breasts and his sigh deepened. He's aroused, she thought. This isn't fear or concern, this is desire. Even as he held her, she felt him strain against his own emotions until he pushed her gently back onto her own ground. She searched his blue eyes and when she didn't find any answers there, she put her hands on either side of his face. They kissed in the hall, falling into each other's arms, but even as he moved his mouth over hers with a soft noise, he grasped each of her wrists and separated himself from her.

He smiled slowly until the dream settled, then shook his head. "The workshop. I should have sent you in here by yourself. Good night, Erin. I'll see you in the morning."

"Kevin, it's all right."

"No, Erin, it's not. This is a breach of trust, manners, ethics, principles, morals..."

She began to laugh. "I must be doing something right."

"You're dangerously vulnerable and far too tempting."

"Was it the socks in my bathing suit or the sight of my naked foot?"

Kevin pointed his finger. "You're supposed to be intimidated, in awe of me, remember? I'm the cranberry baron. Good God, you're staying with me so I can keep you out of harm's way, out of reach and out of trouble."

"Kevin, I don't need a chaperon."

"*I* need the chaperon. You live with my brother for ten months without a hint of that physical pull you talk about. You're in my house for forty-eight hours and I'm kissing you in the hallway."

"My lips started it."

"Erin," he sighed, "could you please be a little less adorable and wide-eyed? You're flirting with things that can get out of control."

"I certainly hope so."

"Erin! You can't just hand a man your heart on a plate. Women who play the way you think you want to..." He paused in the middle of his sentence. "I've never talked to a woman about this, it was always one of my brothers," he mumbled as he gave her a helpless look. "The heart has no place in those kinds of games and neither do you. You're in Millbrook because you're in the beginning of a wonderful career with your whole, bright future ahead of you. Don't mess it up with some meaningless fooling around."

"Have you kept everything inside for so long that you couldn't care? You would be such an easy man to love."

"Erin, I would break your heart."

Seven

Tuesday morning Erin awoke to threatening skies, a perfect match for her disposition. *Meaningless fooling around.* For a man who thought his life was in order, Kevin Branigan had a lot to learn.

He hadn't disturbed her when he'd come back from the barn and the second floor was quiet as she got out of bed. She found his door open, the bed made as she crossed the hall. Avoidance, she thought. It hadn't worked with his trumped-up story about Carol Fraser; perhaps he stood a better chance by staying in the workshop until all hours and rushing back out at dawn. Maybe exhaustion would douse his desire. Erin smiled as she dressed, his response was flattering.

In the hour she had before work, she ran a load of Branigan/O'Connor laundry and made herself a good breakfast. Kevin's bloodstained pants were on top of the hamper so she put them in the set-tub to soak. She ate her cereal on the porch with the dogs at her feet and then hung the wash on the line in the side yard. When she went into the kitchen to return the bowl and pick up her briefcase, Kevin was yawning in front of the coffeemaker.

"How's your foot?" he asked, as she crossed the room with a little limp.

"Not bad at all, I'll soak it again tonight. I didn't see you come in."

"I haven't been out. I moved down the hall to Jody's room and I'll be using the other bathroom, too."

Erin arched her eyebrows against the hurt. "I must be more irresistible than I thought."

"Erin, when you do get around to rational thought, you'll agree this is the best way. I can't be responsible, I don't want to be responsible for another person's feelings."

"Have I asked that of you?"

He sighed and poured his coffee. "Can you trust me enough to believe it would come to that?"

She grabbed her briefcase. "Are all men as conceited as you, Kevin? When you make a pass at a woman, does she warn you against falling in love with her? Love doesn't happen to be on my agenda at the moment, either.

"I left your plate on the counter. Since my heart's not on it, there's plenty of room for a big breakfast. Eat one, you'll need it to keep your strength up," Erin added as she left the house. Kevin Branigan at a loss for a comeback was a rare sight. It gave her the courage to march out to her car without turning back.

Dr. Montgomery was at the clinic for Erin's morning session with the prepared childbirth instructors. Working without interruption, they finished the overview of the program by lunchtime. Erin requested a tour of the labor and delivery facilities at Plymouth General for the afternoon and accepted Sky's invitation to lunch.

They ate on the terrace of the Millbrook Country Club in their business clothes, amid men and women in golf and tennis attire. Although cloudy, it was warm and breezy as Sky talked of the upcoming engagement party. Erin began to think of the dinner dance as another evening with Kevin.

"Kevin and Drew are both members now," Sky was saying, "for business purposes more than anything else. If you could have seen Ryan out there the summer he groomed the greens, Erin, you would have played as much golf and tennis as I did."

"And in spite of all the differences in your backgrounds, there's still going to be a happy ending," Erin added.

"In spite of everything."

From the club, Erin drove to the hospital, had her tour, met with the director of Maternity Services and was back in her makeshift office by four. With what little time remained, she attempted to get her thoughts down on paper but it was close enough to quitting time for her mind to wander. Kevin's rejection and obvious attraction were red flags in front of her eyes, gauntlets at her feet. Because she'd never been burned by love, she saw it all as a thrilling challenge.

That Tuesday afternoon she refused to think about Kevin's words. The idea that the man had felt the need to change bedrooms and leave the house simply widened her grin. She hit the keyboard in front of her and misspelled four words in a row.

Erin pulled her car onto the Bancroft/Branigan lane at five-thirty, feeling as emotionally charged as she had the morning she'd arrived at the clinic. She was ready for the blue eyes and the dark hair and the home cooking. From the hill she could see that the final course of shingles had been added, no doubt a last exhausting push against the threat of rain. However, the only sign of life was Drew on his lawn tractor at the crest of his own property. The Corvette was gone.

"At least someone's glad to see me," she muttered, as she bent to pat Max and let him into the house. There was a note propped on the coffeemaker.

Erin—
Jody's invited you to dinner about seven. Have a great time. See you in the morning,

K.

She began to laugh. A truly desperate man, he was now fixing her up with his brother. She thumbed through the phone directory in the family room and found Branigan, Jas. Jr., Atty sandwiched between Branigan Cranberries and Branigan, Kevin. She dialed the listing for his residence and smiled into the receiver.

"Jody, it's Erin."

"Then you got Kevin's note. I called the clinic after five but the switchboard's off. I was hoping to talk you into a tour of Millbrook and some supper."

"Kevin didn't put you up to this?"

Her honesty seemed to take him back. "No, except that he mentioned your wanting to see more of town."

"And the fact that I had a lot of time on my hands," she added with a laugh. "Thanks for the invitation but I really can't." She explained her fatigue and her foot and her homework and added a fib about Kevin's concern for her entertainment. They said goodbye amiably.

The house smelled of freshly cut grass and the promise of rain as she climbed the stairs and changed into culottes. Her laundry was neatly folded and piled on a corner of the bed.

She put it away before sitting on the edge of the tub to soak her foot. The whine of the sports car and the muffled slam of the screen door below made her heart thump. Kevin was whistling, taking the stairs two at a time. The footsteps stopped abruptly as he reached the landing and she pivoted, lifting her foot from the water.

"Hi," she said as she dabbed the towel on her arch.

"You're home. Wearing that to dinner?"

She looked up at him as he looked down. "Yes. I'm eating downstairs in the kitchen. I'm far too tired and sore to go out and make small talk. You might as well tell me what other diversions you've cooked up for the next four nights so I can cancel them, too. Honestly, Kevin, why don't you just ship me off to one of your brothers' houses?"

"That would have necessitated an explanation."

"But I could have spent the night with Jody?"

"I would have expected you home at a decent hour."

"So that's where Matthew gets his protective instincts."

"Erin, Jody's your type, your age."

"You might have noticed that I'd rather make those kinds of decisions myself. There are just about enough Branigans in my life." She folded the towel and put it back on the rack.

"Have you ever been at a loss for words?" he asked as she passed him.

"I'd like to be. Thanks for folding my laundry."

Kevin cleared his throat. "I didn't know you'd hung it out there this morning. We have a dryer."

"Heat ruins the elastic in my underwear. It didn't rain." She looked at his expression. "Trouble? Holly and Drew hang theirs out."

"They're married."

"Married! You and I have to be married before I can hang my camisole next to your shorts? I shouldn't have put my unmentionables in with yours? It was the only way to make up a full load. I thought you'd be pleased that I'm doing my share."

"Ryan and Sean were pleased, I'll say that."

She began to laugh. "You've been teased! I thought you commanded too much respect for that. Next time I'll string them up here in the bedroom so no one will notice."

"I'll notice," he said under his breath.

"I'd like that," she replied in a voice no louder than his.

"Erin! Occasionally a man, even a man of few words, likes to have the last one."

"I'm sorry, you wanted to say something about my underwear?"

He shook his head and muttered, "Erin, Erin, Erin," as they went down to the kitchen. Once there, he opened the refrigerator and closed it again. "It seems the only way to get you out of the house is to take you myself."

"That's not much of an invitation, but if it has anything to do with the shiny red number out there by the barn, I accept," Erin replied immediately. Twenty minutes later she was being driven through the village with roast beef sandwiches and two ginger ales between them. Daylight was fading and thunder rolled in the distance, but house lights had yet to come on. Sky and Ryan's cars were side by side at Schuyler House and Sean's truck was parked at the fire station. At the far edge of the country club's golf course, Kevin slowed the car and drove it carefully from the paved road to the sandy cartpath edging the cranberry bogs.

"I don't suppose you're taking me parking?" Erin asked as the engine died. "Isn't this where Ryan and Sky started it all?"

"Didn't your mother ever tell you to be subtle, young lady?" He looked horror-struck at what he'd said and touched her arm. "Erin, forgive me, I forgot."

She patted his hand. "It's all right, really. You're so sensitive in so many ways, Kevin. I don't know that my mother would approve of my tactics, but she'd approve of my taste. I miss her, I could use her advice right about now." She busied herself unwrapping the sandwich and when Kevin didn't reply, she looked up at him. "Don't let me make a fool of myself. Please?"

"Desire makes fools of all of us," he whispered as he leaned to her and cupped her face. His lips were warm and when she parted her mouth, his tongue played an ancient game with hers. His chest pressed against her until they parted and stared, brown eyes into blue. Kevin turned and rested his forehead on the steering wheel.

Erin took her sandwich and got out of the car, walking the dike that split the bogs. He came up behind her, carrying the drinks. "I was out here this afternoon. This is the project I mentioned, grading the paths, widening them for better access. The sandpile needs to be moved back; we sand the bogs about every three years during the freeze. The storage shed will go over there where you're looking."

Dusk had reduced the landscape to charcoal gray. She didn't turn until he put his hand under her chin and made her. "Look at me. You aren't foolish, you're sweet and generous and maybe a little headstrong. Your attraction to me is more flattering than you can imagine and if I had less of a conscience we wouldn't be out here right now. But Erin, you mean too much to me, too much to my brothers, for me to take advantage of this situation. The five of them would be at my throat if they thought I'd kissed you the way I just did. Sweetheart, there are a few advantages to age and experience. I'm not trying to keep you from being foolish, but from wasting your specialness. My life's the way I want it; my responsibilities are over. You were meant for roses and love songs. The world is at your feet, and what you feel for me is a prelude to all that.'' He laughed softly. ''You have no idea what you stirred up with your laundry next to mine, what I was accused of.''

''Great. I've got five knights in shining armor and one who's slightly tarnished, all worried about my virtue. For your information, Kevin Branigan, I don't want you to be responsible for me. I'm responsible and my specialness isn't going to be ruined just because I want to share it with you. I've spent six years preparing for a career I adore. I'm in the midst of making that dream into reality. I don't have the time or desire for anything permanent. I don't want roses or love songs. I want the prelude, Kevin. Things are supposed to happen spontaneously between a man and a woman, not be analyzed to death by them.'' She took a breath and looked into his shadowed eyes. ''I wouldn't be talking like this for one minute if I weren't positive that under all that armor and chivalry, you felt the same way I do.''

Eight

———

They returned to the car in silence, broken only by the sound of the opening door. "Keys are in the ignition, Erin, want to drive?"

She smiled at him as she got into the driver's seat. "You're placating me, but I accept." There was no rain, but distant lightning illuminated the horizon as she drove over the country roads. She commented on the excitement and easy handling, then backtracked into Millbrook through its sleeping streets and out toward the homestead.

A dim light in the nursery window was all that shone from Drew and Holly's as Erin drove down the hill. She was seized with the need to postpone entering the house with Kevin, fearing what might happen as much as what might not.

If and when he made love to her, it would be spontaneous, she told herself. There was no denying the spark between them but, begrudgingly, she admitted that his words made sense. She didn't think her mother would have approved of her tactics, not at all.

Kevin was a study in grays as they got out of the car and he bent to greet the dogs as they followed him to the trash barrel in the barn. He threw away the remains of dinner, giving Erin the distinct impression that he was avoiding the house as well.

"Rain's coming. Want to take a walk while it's still dry?" he asked.

"Yes," she replied, although the dropping temperature raised gooseflesh on her bare legs. She snuggled into him as he draped his arm over her shoulder. "Honeysuckle," she murmured as they passed the vines along the garden. "Smells like home, honeysuckle, hay and cow manure."

"You make me think, Erin. You make me analyze everything I feel, everything I'm trying not to feel," Kevin replied, as though he'd heard only his own thoughts.

"We're avoiding that big empty house, aren't we?"

"Yes. I want to kiss you and it's safer out here in the open somehow."

"You're chancing the lightning."

He laughed and pulled her into his chest. "If God were going to strike me with lightning, He'd have done it the very first night. I came home from the dinner with Carol and stayed awake for hours fantasizing about you on the other side of the wall."

"That's quite a confession," she replied, her voice tight, her nerves aflutter.

"You've only made it worse." He bent his head to reach her and their eyes closed together. This time he made no move to stop the exploration as he traced the warmth of her mouth. Lightly, over the thin cotton of her shirt, his hand moved down to the flat plane of her stomach and then up, by inches, until he cupped the soft underside of her breast.

Erin moaned and arched her shoulders as each nipple swelled against the fabric. She leaned into him for balance and every spot her body touched his sent warmth through her. Kevin whispered her name and then let her go.

"This isn't going to help me sleep," he muttered, "and that is what you and I are going to do."

"Sleep," she answered.

"At opposite ends of the hall." He took her hand and started toward the house.

They did just that. They used separate bathrooms and separate bedrooms, calling good-night from opposite ends of the second floor. The wind rose in earnest behind her closed door, flailing the curtains aside and knocking a sheaf of her papers askew on Ryan's desk. She gathered them up after pulling on her nightgown and put in a futile twenty minutes of business time. Thunder rumbled across the sky while she closed the window and Erin stood there looking out at the bogs and the dark shapes of the outbuildings.

She slept under a single sheet in a room grown stuffy from the lack of ventilation. With the windows closed and the door shut, it was still as hot as midday. It wasn't the heat that awoke her, however, but an earsplitting crack. Erin opened her eyes to a room lit bright as day and then suddenly dark and she sat up, her hand over her heart.

The sound of Kevin's running made her turn and as she heard him hurry into his own room another bolt, closer still, illuminated their fifty acres. Sean and Anne's house flashed before her eyes as a jagged streak of lightning slammed into their roof. Erin's hand was already on the closet door where she grabbed the first thing she felt and threw it over her brief gown. She got to Kevin's room as he was snapping on the light and lifting his bedside phone.

"Don't use the phone, it's too dangerous," she cried.

He ignored her and tapped out a number. "Annie, it's Kevin. Damn right I saw it. You lit up like a Christmas tree. You're sure? Okay, take care of the kids, I can hear them crying from here. I love you, too. Good night." When the receiver was back in the cradle, his shoulders sagged. He took deep, ragged breaths and then looked up at Erin. "Sean got off his shift at eleven, he's home. Their lightning rods worked. Scared the life out of the girls, but the house is fine." His composure was returning and he stifled a grin.

"Erin O'Connor, what on earth are you wearing?"

"Something of Ryan's I grabbed in the dark," she replied, looking down at a pajama top that hung five inches off her fingertips and fell just above her knee-length gossamer sleepwear. "I'm sure you don't believe it, but I have some sense of modesty. I thought this might keep you from lusting after me in case you had to choose between that and putting out a house fire."

"Very thoughtful. Let's see if it will keep down my lust long enough to get you back to bed. Seriously, are you all right?"

She thought seriously of feigning terror to see how far it got her. "Frightened but fine," she replied as they entered her darkened room. "I don't suppose you'll have any trouble getting back to sleep."

"No more than usual."

They turned to the window as rain began to pelt against the panes, filling the void left by their silence. She licked her lower lip and listened to her heart as it thumped wildly against her ribs.

"This evens the score," he whispered, dangerously close to her ear. "You did promise to appear in your nightgown after you surprised me at the sink."

"Yes...I did. It's only fair." She hardly dared to breathe as he put his fingers inside the lapels of her makeshift robe. His knuckles grazed her skin and he hesitated. "Erin?" he whispered.

"Kevin, the answer is *yes*." When he'd lifted his brother's pajama top from her shoulders, she looked up at him, feeling his eyes skim the little she wore underneath.

"I'm too old to be deflowering almost-virgins."

"Apparently not," she murmured as she kissed his chest.

"It's too late in my life for a permanent relationship." She put her fingertips over his heart as he spoke and sighed as he played with her hair.

"It's too early in mine," was her answer.

"My brothers'd shoot me at dawn for my thoughts alone. If they ever suspected me of this, there'd be hell to pay."

"I'll be back in Boston Sunday night with no one the wiser," she replied, surprised at the length of his silence.

"And protection, Erin?"

"That's my line of work, Kevin, I even thought of that."

He kissed her forehead. "You know the earth doesn't always move the first time around. These things take practice. I don't want you to worry."

She *was* beginning to worry. Self-consciousness made her aware of the speed of her pulse and how badly she wanted to be perfect for him. When the thunder rolled again, it drew their attention to the window, and they were bathed in a flash of light. As the grumbling rolled away, Kevin lifted Erin into his arms and moved toward the bed.

"The last time I carried you, you had a roofing nail in your foot."

She nuzzled his neck. "I'll take your arms around me anyway I can."

Kevin lowered her to her feet and they stood at the edge of the bed. "I may hate myself in the morning. This is the most selfish thing I've ever done." He shook his head. "All these nights I've fantasized myself into a state worse than puberty dreaming of holding you."

"And you think I need roses and love songs? Just the thought that you fantasize about me would keep me warm all winter." Her voice fell away as Kevin touched the strap on her shoulder. She held her breath and closed her eyes, clasping her icy fingers tightly.

"Erin, can you relax?" he whispered.

She shook her head, grateful for the fullness of her hair and the deep shadows in the room. He laughed softly and her cheeks burned. "Where's the woman with the caustic wit and the sexy innuendos?" he asked.

"Out of her league," she mumbled, horrified to hear her teeth chatter.

"Shall I go? Would you like a brandy?"

She shook her head as Kevin gently pushed his fingers into her hair and tilted her face. "It's only me, just the two of us, Erin. There's no right or wrong way to any of this. Trust yourself, trust me."

"I do," she replied as he bent his head and kissed her. Her mouth opened to his and he lingered, tracing her lips with his tongue, massaging her temples and the nape of her neck with strong, leisurely strokes. Kevin made no attempt to remove her nightgown—he didn't even touch her shoulders or the bare expanse of her back—yet every movement of his hands in her hair and his lips over hers warmed her. Her trembling stopped, replaced by a swaying which brought her against him. The only indication that restraint might have been involved was the moan that broke from his throat as her gossamer-covered breasts pressed against his chest.

She tightened her own fingers at the back of his head and she kissed him deeply, finding his tongue, matching his exploration with her own. Pleasure radiated through her, intensified at every point where his skin touched hers. She was unaware of Kevin's patience as he guided her through a haze of sensation, letting her initiate the progression.

As if in a dream, she felt his mouth on her eyelids, the bridge of her nose, back across her parted lips. He rested his hands on the straps at her bodice again, hesitated, then moved down to her hips. His splayed fingers cupped her bottom and she opened her eyes, searching his. What he saw in her face must have pleased and reassured him, for he smiled slowly, then closed his eyes and brought her hand to him. "Erin," he moaned as she released the drawstring at his waist.

She gasped softly as he kicked the pajamas aside and lay back on the bed, still smiling. His skin was warm, dry, velvet smooth as she opened her palms and let sensation radiate from the pads of her fingers into her heart.

As she stroked, the desire spiraling inside her began to spin in widening circles, building as the gathering storm had moments earlier. Kevin coaxed and encouraged, but as his self-control ebbed, his conversation dissolved to the sweet murmur of *yes*, when he pulled her down to him.

Erin was mesmerized by his desire for her, a confirmation of everything that she'd suspected. His fingers trembled as he finally slid the nightgown from her shoulders. "It's my turn," he whispered. He kissed her deeply, hungrily as his hands traveled over her breasts, cupping the softness, then massaging each between fingers and thumb. Erin was never still as she tried to keep her own hands in safe places but the more Kevin touched her the more sensually charged every place she touched seemed to be.

She whispered his name and pulled his head to her breasts. He touched her first, and as her hands guided him, she felt his tension build. She was drunk with the feel of him against her as his fingers followed the primitive rhythm, made perfect by the sudden weight as their bodies melded. Erin wrapped herself around him, deepening his pleasure, feeling him lose himself to sensation. "Catch up," he gasped as he tried in vain to slow the pace.

His embrace locked heartbeat to heartbeat and beneath him she matched his hunger. Erin clung to him, overwhelmed by the joy in his voice as he whispered her name. She wouldn't let him stop and when she knew that he couldn't, her satisfaction came from the knowledge that she was the source of his ecstasy.

She felt his joy tear through him, up from the well of desire in which they'd plunged. His roughness dissolved to undulating pressure, his handsome features a mirror of what he felt. She absorbed his shudder, felt the kiss on her face. Gradually, as if emerging from a dream, Kevin shifted and relaxed, cupping her breast in the afterglow. He started to whisper something, but she pressed her fingers to his lips. "Sleep, it was perfect," she murmured.

When she awoke it was still raining, the dawn no more than dim, gray light. She was being eased from sleep by the pressure of Kevin's body as he held her. She stretched into a yawn that changed to a moan as tender places pressed against him. A yearning sensation danced under her skin, deepened by the frustration of having come so close.

She watched Kevin open his eyes, watched the slow smile. He knows, she thought. Without a word he made love to her at half the pace of the first time, exploring the flat plane of her stomach, the inner curve of her thighs, the nape of her neck. She listened to the rain slacken and then lost all track as her desire gathered in bottomless pools.

When his touch grew intimate, he traced the shell of her ear with his tongue. "Good morning," he sighed, his breath catching as she began to respond. This time they raced together until Erin felt nothing but the incredible fire engulfing her and the need for Kevin to quench it. This was what he felt, she thought, as her senses responded to his lightest touch. She trusted him with everything she was, let him lead her until he said, "Now, Erin," and the welcome weight returned.

In long drawn-out moments of pleasure she drew everything from him, only dimly aware that the more she took the more she gave. They soared, together this time, until passion broke. Contentment soothed her as feminine satisfaction replaced the yearning. She touched his cheek when they were finally still. "It's about time I got hit by lightning," she said, and nuzzled back against him.

They showered together in the morning, teasing as they shared the soap. Erin shampooed her hair and raised her face to the spray. "Do you think the lightning bolt did any damage last night?"

Kevin kissed her shoulder. "From what I can tell, you seemed to enjoy it as much as I did."

"Kevin," she protested mildly.

"Oh, you meant Anne and Sean's house. They're well grounded, but I'll take a look this morning."

Her heart warmed at the memory of his concern on the phone and his comforting "I love you, too" to his sister-in-law. For four more days a little bit of this would be hers to share. How ironic that she'd worked so hard at making Kevin understand the depth of her feelings and now, after one perfect night, she felt the need to hide them.

She had prepared herself, protected herself. What she had failed to anticipate was the vulnerability exposed by their intimacy. She found herself longing for some nebulous assurance from Kevin, some off-hand patter as reassuring as his "I love you, too" must have been to Anne. Erin stepped from the stall and wrapped herself in a towel as though the rough terry cloth could shield her from her own feelings.

Kevin followed and did the same, glancing at the mirrored vanity. "For future reference, let the men in your life shave before you shower. It steams up the mirror so they can't see."

"I'll remember that," she replied as she crossed the hall to her bedroom. His pointed use of the plural stabbed at her and she was too caught up in that vulnerability to suspect that his own defenses might be at work.

Wednesday, the stormy weather that had spent all of Tuesday developing, dissipated further. The rain stopped for good by noon and the brisk sou'east wind shoved the storm farther inland. With Childbirth Preparation behind her, Erin tackled demographic reports and files from the Department of Social Services and Ryan's Police League. The board was already convinced of the need for parenting courses, but Erin's goal was to convince them of the necessity for a twofold approach. Teenage mothers lacking nutritional information and routine skills should comprise one group, while parents unable to cope with the stress of child rearing, risking abuse or neglect were to be part of another. The job of encouraging Marnie Taylor to press for funding for two programs was left to Erin and took up what was left of the afternoon.

By the time she headed back to the bogs, the sun had broken through the last of the clouds in the evening sky. She wondered as she walked from her car to the house if she would always associate the sweet summer smell of wet earth with her first night in Kevin's arms. However, doubt paralyzed her on the steps of the porch in the midst of her reminiscing. Now what? Where on this fresh wet earth was the uninhibited flirt who so blatantly enjoyed the chase? What came next? Who was to make the first move now?

With any luck at all, she would open the screen door and Kevin would greet her in the nude with a "Hi, love, let's go up to bed.'' Then she'd know exactly what he was thinking and what he had in mind. She prayed that he'd give her some signals she could read.

She put her hand against the rising butterflies in her stomach and pulled back the door. The kitchen was empty and she found Kevin in the family room with a drink, mulling over a technical paper on pest control from the Ocean Spray Cooperative. ''Welcome home,'' he murmured. ''Hang on just a sec, I've got one more paragraph.'' He was coming through loud and clear.

Erin sank into the couch cushions and put her feet up on the coffee table, waiting until he finished. When he slapped the paper at her feet she smiled at him. ''Hi.''

''Hi. You look as beat as I feel, although considering our lack of sleep, I'd say we're remarkable.''

She felt better and when he tugged her up onto her feet and into a hug, it was better still. ''I've got your dinner ready,'' he said. ''I've eaten. Drew and Ryan are coming over to discuss the project out on the bogs I showed you last night.''

She considered attempting to get him out of his clothes before they arrived, but Kevin was already pulling a plate from the microwave. Didn't he know that she needed to hear some reference to everything else he'd shown her last night? Insight was coming to Erin at odd moments and now, as he handed her the dinner plate, she realized just how young and inexperienced she really was. Kevin had recognized that, and had tried to shield her from *this*. It hadn't been the physical intimacy that worried him, but the aftermath, the dopey, besotted, moonstruck euphoria she was left to deal with while he went blissfully on with his life.

"Tell me about your day," he said pleasantly, as he pulled out the chair next to hers.

"I'm trying to develop parenting courses," she replied, looking at the man whose blasé physical relationships had probably spanned close to twenty years. Hers was approaching twenty hours. She cleared her throat. "Kevin, I hope you and your brothers will consider supporting the clinic. I know Branigan Cranberries underwrites a performance of the Plymouth Orchestra. You could do even more good by helping fund social services."

"Sky's been after us, too. We'll give it some thought."

Before they could continue, Drew arrived in the kitchen with Ryan right behind him. There was some small talk about the storm and questions about her day, even teasing about her host and the underwear incident. Before she finished dinner, however, they excused themselves and moved into the office off the front hall.

When she'd finished, she went upstairs to change, listening to the low masculine voices as she climbed the stairs. She shook out her hair and pulled on some jeans, stopping briefly at the office door as she came back down. They all turned their heads expectantly.

"I'm going to run over and see Holly for a while, then spend some time at the desk in my room," Erin said. "I've got to put together a proposal. Ryan, your desk has been a great help."

"My pleasure. Sky and I want you to come to dinner Saturday. It will be your last night in Millbrook. We'll see you then."

She thanked him and wondered if the old Erin would have made a sly reference to the use of Ryan's pajama top, and if it would have made any of them blush. The perky, bold innocent seemed gone for good as she glanced once at Kevin. "Thank you for dinner. I'll let you get back to work. Good night."

"Good night, love," he replied, raising his head as both his brothers arched their eyebrows.

Nine

Love, ha,'' she replied hastily and sarcastically. "He keeps accusing me of stepping on his homemaking abilities. Your brother's a cantankerous old bachelor who can't stand anyone else doing his laundry.''

"Bossy little thing,'' Kevin added. "Tried to take over the minute her suitcase was down.''

Erin wrinkled her nose. "You might do well with a woman's touch around here, if you could find one to put up with you.'' She left them laughing.

After an hour with Holly, she returned to the house, but the men were deep in discussion with the door partially closed so she went up to her room without disturbing them.

She lost herself in her work until her lids began to close and when her head nodded twice at the desk, she admitted defeat and gave in to fatigue. Would Kevin expect to find her waiting? Was that presumptuous? Did these games have rules? And why, she berated herself, did they suddenly seem like *Kevin's* rules?

She got into bed with a sigh, behind her closed door. She was awakened by Branigan voices; one of the brothers had come upstairs with Kevin. Fully alert, she lay under the sheet and listened to their muffled conversation until sleep overtook her.

When she awoke again, the sun was up and she was stabbed by disappointment. You got what you were after, O'Connor, she thought. After all, this is Kevin's house and Kevin, most definitely, is calling the shots. She washed up quickly, intending to dress and put on her makeup in the bedroom, but as she scurried back across the hall, the second bedroom door opened.

Kevin lounged against the jamb, audaciously dressed in cotton, pinstripe pajama bottoms no more substantial than handkerchief fabric. Determined to appear casual herself, Erin tossed her head and straightened her shoulders.

"My God, I love it when you do that," Kevin murmured.

She blinked. For a fraction of a second they eyed each other and then she turned away. "Sleep well?" she asked, moving to her bedroom.

"Not particularly."

"Maybe you were in the wrong bed."

"Was I? Your closed door said differently."

"Kevin, I'm a little new at this and we *are* in your house."

He stretched, pushing his arms up over his head, his chest muscles tightening and the drawstring at his waist taking a jaunty slide. "A man likes an occasional invitation, Erin. Has to do with ego and confidence, I guess."

A smile played at the corners of her mouth. "I'll remember that for future reference—that and not steaming up the bathroom mirror. You are full of advice, Mr. Branigan. I've enjoyed following it." She also enjoyed the change in her mood, ignoring, for the moment, the fact that thirty seconds in Kevin's presence had been responsible.

He walked to the bathroom and called over his shoulder, "You might also remember that when you're trying to make a point, you'll be more successful dressed in something more like Ryan's pajama top than that little slip of temptation."

Witty words, banter...they were back on her ground. "Well, my goodness," she replied from across the hall, "why don't you come over here and help me remove the temptation?" He did and since it left no time for breakfast, Erin went to work with an empty stomach, satisfied nevertheless.

Time began to fly. Erin found herself enjoying the hectic pace at the clinic for more than professional reasons. She was too busy to dwell on her desire to be wrapped in Kevin's arms, and her consultation took all her energy and most of her concentration until the end of the day. Then the staff would trickle home and the fever would start. Intimate reverie would seep into her head. In midsentence her fingers would stop typing and she'd pause with them suspended over the keyboard. Her nerves danced and a flush might creep up from her collar. She drove out to the bogs as if she had no time to spare and made love to Kevin as if she had all the time in the world.

Although he was as anxious as she to lose himself in their passion, he seemed amused by Erin's constant enthusiasm and curiosity. Her confidence grew. She was sure of her role as the week progressed, sure of his delight in her and involved enough in her work to know that she would be able to leave Millbrook and the cranberry baron with her heart intact.

Erin went into Kevin's arms the moment her briefcase hit the floor, snuggling against him as he tugged the barrettes from her hair. They made love in his bed or hers before dinner with nothing covering them but long shafts of the late summer sun.

Long after they lay still she'd murmur to him, question him, probe his silence. She marvelled that he could give himself physically with such abandon yet sequester all but the surface of his emotions. It told Erin more about his previous relationships than he ever would have offered. Gradually, however, his smile, his painless recollections grew. They'd talk cranberry business, barn construction, then move into long-forgotten anecdotes. It was as precious to her as the lovemaking.

Early Thursday evening, Kevin lay on his back watching the breeze blow back the curtains as a heat wave hovered over the bogs. Their flesh glistened as Erin walked her fingers over his chest. "Who's your favorite woman?"

"Good Lord, Erin," he said.

"I mean Branigan woman, counting Sky, who's practically one already."

He rolled on his side and looked over her shoulder at the view. "That's a loaded question. They're all unique, but each one's suited to the man she wound up with. Annie's the earth mother, steady and settled and Sean's touchstone. Sky's the aristocrat, gorgeous, flamboyant, but she gets more out of Ryan with one of those smiles than I ever could with bribes, threats or promises. Holly's the surprise. She pulled us all together *against* her, fell in love with Drew, then the next thing I knew, she was activating Bittersweet Bogs and forcing us all to pull *with* her." He looked back at Erin and sat up against the headboard. "Erin, you should have been here during the storm when she went into labor. There's not much that scares me anymore, but that's one night I'd rather not have to relive. If anything had happened..."

She put her fingers on his lips. "Nothing did. Babies are born, Kevin, when they're good and ready. You weren't any more responsible for that night than you are for their lives today."

"It's a hard habit to break."

Friday at the clinic was so hectic, Erin thought of nothing but the programs she'd arranged and the staff she'd trained. Marnie, Winnie and Sky took her to lunch and she made her final presentation to the board members at a four o'clock meeting. And then it was over. She'd left them trained and confident, better for having shared her knowledge and expertise. She'd met the challenge, given them her best effort and was finished with what she'd set out to do. The parallels in her private life weren't lost to her. Kevin Branigan had done as much for her as she'd done for the clinic.

The only challenge left to her was getting through Saturday, a full day with his family, as if she were still nothing more than a houseguest. "So, Erin, it's over," Kevin said blithely as they ate breakfast. "Was it worth it?"

The double entendre lingered between them as she looked across the table into his thoughtful expression. "I came down here with some goals in mind and I met them—both of them."

"Your independence will serve you well," he answered.

"Based on your experience?"

"My independence is important to me, Erin."

Erin's smile was just short of patronizing. Because his house was now empty, he felt he'd achieved the solitude never possible before, she thought. Out loud she replied, "Kevin, your love and responsibility to your family are as much a part of you as your spine or your heart." She paused, looked deep into his slate-blue eyes and when she saw that he acknowledged the truth in her comment, she put her hand on his shoulder. "What you feel for people—what you try to deny you feel sometimes—won't fade simply because the bedrooms aren't occupied. I pushed and flirted my way into your heart this week, but you let it happen. We both know that if you'd sat me down and told me to stop, I would have. It was a prelude for me, a wonderful one and maybe an encore for you." She laughed softly. "All week I've looked at the concern in your eyes, your worry that I'd fall in love with you. I do love you, Kevin, for everything you've given me. I'll never forget any of it. In fact, when I do fall in love for good, he'll probably have lots of the same qualities. Get rid of the concerned expression, Kevin, I'm just fine, in fact I'm just about perfect and that should polish your ego till it shines!"

The look between them lingered, however, and Erin got up from the table, plate in hand. A splinter of pain settled deep beneath her breastbone but she couldn't give herself the luxury of hoping she might have misread his expression. She knew better than to cling to the possibility that Kevin would correct her.

He got up from the table as well, and brought his plate to the counter. "It's been an unforgettable week," he replied. "It'll be nice to have you back for the engagement party."

"I'm looking forward to it," she said as she rinsed the dishes.

"Erin?"

She turned from the sink.

"It's been a long time since anyone 'pushed and flirted' her way into my bed. I'm still not comfortable with the idea that I let it happen, but you have a way..." He raked his hair with his fingers. "You'll be missed, love."

"So will you."

Drew and Holly chose that moment to appear, babe in arms, at the door to suggest some tennis at the club. Kevin agreed so readily Erin was left with the unmistakable impression that he felt there was a need to keep her occupied—and in the company of others. It was the beginning of a day in which Kevin and Erin played the roles of platonic host and houseguest to the hilt. It was a role thrust on her and the splinter of pain remained. It helped to remind her that she'd gotten everything she'd wanted, and taken even more than had been offered. She'd played house for a week and the week was over.

Their morning of mixed doubles was followed by the return to the bogs and the arrival of Jody, Sean and Anne. Even if either Erin or Kevin had had anything intimate on their minds, the open house atmosphere would have made it impossible.

At the end of the day they emerged from their separate rooms casually dressed for dinner at Schuyler House with Sky and Ryan. The first floor of the historic house was finished, impeccably restored and furnished. The four of them had drinks in the cozy library, toured the rooms and grilled and ate dinner on the brick terrace in the back garden. It was almost everything Erin would have wished for in a final evening in Millbrook.

"Did you get to drive Kevin's toy?" Sky asked over dessert.

Erin laughed. "I did. I dropped so many hints, and pleaded and begged so obnoxiously that he had to give in. We went out to the bogs by the golf course and looked at the plans for grading and adding storage sheds. *I* wanted Kevin to show me the historic spot where you two started it all. He wanted to show me the sprinkler system."

Kevin gave her a sideways glance. "I'm thinking of having a historic marker made as a wedding present," he said to Sky. *"On this site, unbeknownst to Kevin Branigan, one August night his younger brother and a Boston debutante started it all."*

Ryan clasped Kevin's shoulder. "You might add that thirteen years later I fished her out of the bogs not a hundred yards to the west."

"And the romance was reborn," Erin sighed teasing. "The very idea gives me goose bumps."

"You should have seen the size of mine! I was freezing and soaked and there was Officer Branigan, about the handsomest thing I'd ever seen in or out of a uniform," Sky said, kissing her fiancé's cheek.

Kevin yawned. "I have a suspicion I'm going to be hearing this story for the next fifty years. Ryan, I can't think of a thing you've done to deserve the likes of Sky, but I don't mind admitting defeat."

Sky turned her attention to Kevin. "Your problem, Big Brother, is that you have no sense of romance. Although, I do recall seeing a tear or two in those Branigan blue eyes when you finally got Drew, Holly and the baby off to the hospital after the delivery."

"That was just fatigue," he mumbled.

Sky looked at Erin and grinned. "You've been his guest all week, think there's any hope?"

Erin tried not to look startled, answering too quickly, "None. He's a cranky, old bachelor set in his ways. He does tend to come to life about dinnertime, and can be pleasant company at the end of the day when he puts his mind to it, but the rest of the time it's just work, work, work."

Conversation got no more serious than that and amid promises to return for the engagement party, Erin said her goodbyes with Kevin. It was nearly midnight when they walked to the Corvette in the driveway. She put out her open

.. be tempted!

See inside for special
4 FREE BOOKS offer

 Silhouette Desire™

Discover deliciously different romance with 4 Free Novels from

Silhouette Desire™

Sit back and enjoy four exciting romances—yours **FREE** from Silhouette Books! But wait . . . there's *even more* to this great offer! You'll also get . . .

A COMPACT MANICURE SET—ABSOLUTELY FREE! You'll love your beautiful manicure set—an elegant and useful accessory to carry in your handbag. Its rich burgundy case is a perfect expression of your style and good taste—and it's yours free with this offer!

PLUS A FREE MYSTERY GIFT—A surprise bonus that will delight you!

You can get all this just for trying Silhouette Desire!

MONEY-SAVING HOME DELIVERY!

Once you receive your 4 FREE books and gifts, you'll be able to preview more great romance reading in the convenience of your own home at less than retail prices. Every month we'll deliver 6 brand-new Silhouette Desire novels right to your door months before they appear in stores. If you decide to keep them, they'll be yours for only $2.24 each! That's 26¢ less per book than what you pay in stores—with no additional charges for home delivery!

SPECIAL EXTRAS—FREE!

You'll also get our monthly newsletter, packed with news of your favorite authors and upcoming books—FREE! And as a valued reader, we'll be sending you additional free gifts from time to time—as a token of our appreciation.

BE TEMPTED! COMPLETE, DETACH AND MAIL YOUR POSTPAID ORDER CARD TODAY AND RECEIVE 4 FREE BOOKS, A MANICURE SET AND A MYSTERY GIFT—PLUS LOTS MORE!

A FREE
Manicure Set
and Mystery Gift *await you, too!*

Keep and mail this prepaid card today!-2

Silhouette Desire™

Silhouette Books
901 Fuhrmann Blvd., P.O. Box 9013, Buffalo, NY 14240-9963

☐ **YES!** Please rush me my four Silhouette Desire novels with my FREE Manicure Set and Mystery Gift, as explained on the opposite page. I understand that I am under no obligation to purchase any books. The free books and gifts remain mine to keep.   225 CIY JAX8

_____
NAME   (please print)

_____
ADDRESS   APT.

_____
CITY   STATE   ZIP

Offer limited to one per household and not valid for present subscribers.
Prices subject to change.

PRINTED IN U.S.A.

palm. "What's a girl have to do to get the keys to your car one last time?"

"Behave yourself," he muttered, "you'll be gone tomorrow, I'm the one who'll have to live with the innuendos you threw around."

Erin took the keys and when they were both in the car, she turned on the ignition. "I've behaved myself for twenty-four years. If there's anything I've learned from you this week, it's how to let go and enjoy yourself."

Kevin sighed and leaned back. "I'll say this, it won't be the same around here without you."

"Goodness, I should hope not."

When she'd parked the car in the courtyard, she and Kevin walked slowly toward the empty house. "It's a beautiful night, shall we walk the dogs?" she asked, looking out at the dark geometric bogs.

"Would you rather wait upstairs for me?"

"It's still warm and I love it out here."

Kevin whistled for Max and Domino and when they trotted ahead, he put his arm across Erin's shoulder, drawing her next to him, matching her stride. "You do love it, I watched that in you all week. You're a country girl, Marlborough Street or not."

"True enough."

They fell into their usual silence and traversed the cartpath, heading toward the woodlands that formed the far border of the property. Moonlight glistened off the pond and Sean's house stood as a dark sentinel. At the edge of the pines they stopped and moved with gestures each had grown to anticipate. She wanted his hands in her hair, knew he craved the pressure of her fingers in the small of his back. Arousal began in both lovers before the first kiss ended.

"Let's go back, love," Kevin sighed against her temple.

Erin played with the buttons of his polo shirt. "In all these years, have you ever snuck away out here, right under your brothers' noses?"

"I used to sneak cigarettes over there by the pump."

She shook her head. "Back when you were my age, was there ever a girl, like Sky, somebody who tempted you to be spontaneous, and careless?" As she talked, she pulled his shirt from his waistband. "Have you ever been reckless Kevin, hiding from your brothers the way they hid from you?"

Gently, he put his hands on her wrists. "I've always been partial to beds."

She began to play with his belt buckle and he suddenly tightened his grip. "Kevin, you never snuggled out here in the darkness with anyone and taught her all about the fine art of seduction?"

"Erin, you have nothing left to learn!"

"Anyone," she repeated, now on tiptoes at his ear. "Anyone but me?"

He gasped in surprise as she parted the buckle and pushed the button through its hole. The involuntary swaying of their hips brushed his khaki against her madras sundress. "Never out here, of course not," he growled. "Let's go back. God, I want you when you're like this."

She kept her fingers moving in the millimeters that separated them. "I think I owe it to Drew and Sean and Ryan, maybe even Jody and Matt. This is my swan song, Kevin, and I intend to go out in style. You've taught me everything, now, please, let me give you something *you've* never done."

She hadn't felt Kevin fight his desire since their first days together. She laughed softly and stepped away from him, deeper into the privacy of the woods. Thick mats of pine needles crackled as she sank to her knees and stealthily slid the zipper of her dress down over her spine. He knelt down to her and tried to bring her to her feet, but the straps tumbled off her shoulders and the bodice off her breasts. "This is the best way I know to say thank you," she whispered as he bent his head and the kisses began.

Ten

When they finally returned to the house, Erin spent the last night in Kevin's bed and awoke in the morning to find him lying beside her, twirling a pine needle between his fingers.

"This was in your hair," he said.

"A memento. I think we deserve our own historic marker, don't you?"

His sigh was deep, contented. "You are an amazing woman. I've fought my own instincts with everything I had and even that wasn't enough."

"Maybe this was easy for us because we knew there was an end to it. One perfect week not to be spoiled by silly attempts at keeping the intensity alive with so much distance between us. I put in long days, teach at night. You're locked into a business that needs your time and attention right here. My goodness, Kevin, don't I sound adult? My first love affair and I've come out of it free of guilt or expectations that neither of us could hope to live up to."

Kevin bent to her. "I love you for that."

She kissed him. "I love you for this."

They filled the morning with ordinary tasks. She showered and packed, stripped the beds and ran a wash. Kevin mowed the lawn and weeded the vegetable garden. After putting her luggage in her car, she found him staring into the honeysuckle vines. "I should get rid of these," he blurted when he realized he was being observed.

Erin looked at the cultivated potato hills and the straight rows of beet tops. "My things are in the car. I folded your laundry and left it on top of the dryer."

Kevin nodded. "Stay for lunch?"

"No," she replied, offering vague hospital, consultation report excuses.

"It's going to be a scorcher, how about a swim?"

"I'd have to borrow your socks and Anne's suit again. No, this is goodbye time, Kevin."

His penetrating gaze settled into her brown eyes. "Erin, will you be all right?"

Because I spent four days living like a newlywed, playing house with Millbrook's most confirmed bachelor? she wanted to reply. Instead she scoffed. "Have I given you any other impression?"

"No, love, you haven't."

"Well, then, you see?" She cut the reply in midsentence, horrified to hear the catch in her voice.

"Stay tonight. Go back in the morning. We need to talk," Kevin began, but Drew and Holly were making their way down the driveway.

"You're not a talker and you know it. It's time to get back to reality. Stop looking so guilty," she whispered as the other family members came within earshot.

They all saw her off with waves and goodbyes and hugs. She kissed Kevin on the cheek. Erin looked once into the rearview mirror at the family lined up and waving; honked and bounced her way out the Branigan/Bancroft lane. Her composure held until she skirted the village and passed the bogs. The sob she'd held in so tightly tore from her throat as she passed the golf course, but still she managed to drive, wiping at the tears with the back of her arm. When she could no longer focus on the road and she was safely beyond the Millbrook limits, Erin pulled over to the shoulder and pressed her open palms over her face.

Erin—
Welcome home. My attempt at meatloaf is in the fridge. I'll try to be home by six, if not, eat without me. Delivered baby #1 last night. Fantastic!!!
                                                    XXX, Matt

The note sat with a letter from Nancy and one from her father. Erin took them with her to her room, unpacked and tried to concentrate on the news from London and the gossip from Warren County. Think positively, she demanded of herself. At least the affair had been in Millbrook and she wasn't left with a hundred maudlin memories every time she looked around the apartment.

The heat shimmered and rose from Marlborough Street and Erin turned on the living room fan. Even the whir of the motor wasn't enough to block out the sound of rock music from the alley. She peered out at three students on the fire escape with their beers and box. Over the general traffic she heard the sirens from the Boylston Street fire station. Had it always been so loud? Would every racing fire truck remind her of Sean and his older brother?

She put the meatloaf in the oven at five and at six Matt kept his word and came home for the night. His newfound enthusiasm for his Obstetrics and Gynecology rotation was her saving grace. He entertained her with tales of the delivery room and maternity floor. Their shared knowledge gave Erin the common ground she needed to focus on his week rather than hers.

When it was his turn to listen, Erin gave him a detailed account of her successes at the clinic and her determination to have Millbrook offer two parenting programs. "This is a milestone for you, Erin," Matt replied. "The more consulting you do, the better."

She shrugged. "This time around was painless. I had your house and your brothers for diversion. Working from a suitcase in a motel room wouldn't have the same appeal."

"And how were the diversions?"

She ignored the internal *thump.* "Wonderful! I swam in the pond, got to know your nieces and your dogs. Kevin made me feel right at home. I was treated as family; it was lovely. I miss the solitude already. It's loud back here!"

Matt seemed to relax. "Good. I'm glad Kevin didn't leave you high and dry and go chasing after his own social life. The solitude gets old fast, believe me."

Erin began her old routine the next morning, putting in long hours and catching up on what she'd missed at the hospital. Matt was as busy as he'd ever be with the OB/GYN rotation, unable to predict whether he'd be home or not. With Nancy gone until fall, Erin made a determined effort to perk up her social life, trying not to dwell on the yearning for the evening routine Kevin had established. To come home to dinner and somebody's arms had never been missed until Kevin had let her experience it. The void it left widened as the days passed.

She missed his massaging her neck and the feel of his shoulder muscles under her fingers. She missed coaxing him to talk and the resulting conversation. He'd been the greatest challenge of her life and a lot of the rest of it was beginning to pale in comparison.

Erin O'Connor, however, was not one to wallow in melancholy. She prescribed for herself a healthy dose of time away from 319 Marlborough Street, met friends for dinner and nurses for breakfast. It helped. Thursday morning before she left for the eleven-to-four shift, she crossed paths with an exhausted Matt, struggling into the apartment in search of sleep. The phone rang as he collapsed into a chair. "I'll get it," he mumbled as Erin finished her toast.

"Kevin, how are you?" he asked drowsily. Erin's heart gave an involuntary leap. "Can't, I'm exhausted. Don't know, I'll ask." Matt looked across the room at her. "Kevin's got two tickets for the Sox game tonight, want to give it a try?"

"Sure, why not?" she replied. Her palms began to perspire. What was this, a house call to make sure she had her equilibrium back? She was supposed to sit through an evening and kiss him good-night on the stoop? Lost in her tangled thoughts and emotions, Erin left Matt and went to the bathroom to brush her teeth. When she returned, ready for work, he'd hung up.

"All set," he called cheerfully, heading for his bed. "I'll leave him a key and he'll be here when you get home. I offered him Nancy's room tonight, so he doesn't have to fight the traffic to the Cape."

"You didn't!"

Matt turned from his doorway. "Problem?" He narrowed his gaze. "Erin, come to think of it, you've hardly mentioned him. He didn't—"

"Go to bed, Matthew. No, he didn't. I was simply thinking that these are smaller quarters than the house in Millbrook, that's all." Erin O'Connor wasn't simply thinking anything at all. She was emoting, yearning, pining, fighting the all-too-familiar spiral of desire already starting to spin beneath her crisp white uniform. She wasn't at all thrilled with what the mere mention of the man's name was capable of doing to her.

It was one thing to have talked him into a whirlwind week in Millbrook. *This* kind of loopy, adolescent behavior, just when she was putting it behind her... All right, she admitted, putting it behind her was worse than she'd ever imagined. "Never mind," she muttered out loud, determined to find herself a date for Friday night, just as soon as the cranberry baron went back to his bogs.

At the hospital she had to force herself to concentrate. She found herself contemplating the lives of her patients, wondering about their families, their marriages. She studied the husbands who visited and noted the amount of support they offered their recuperating wives. She watched the way they held their children and for the first time in her life, Erin compared her circumstances to theirs.

At four she took the train to Copley Square, came up from the subway to diminished sunshine and stopped for groceries on the way home. She rounded the corner of her block of Marlborough and looked at the figure casually draped across her front steps. Two weeks earlier, she might have had trouble discerning which Branigan was studying the Victorian town houses. Not today.

She shifted the bag in her arms and worked her way along the sidewalk. He turned, recognized her and got to his feet. He'll put his hands in his pockets, she thought. He'll stand there smiling that smile and jangling change.

Kevin stepped from the stoop to the sidewalk and slipped his hands into his pockets. His smile was slow and easy, full of expectation. She hated herself for the intimate knowledge, and hated him for being so damned disconcerting.

"Hi," he said when she'd arrived at his feet.

"Hi," she replied with all the aplomb of their first walk down this street.

He picked up his small overnight case. "I hadn't planned on staying until Matt made the offer."

"Afraid there wouldn't be much point if Matt were here?" Erin fumbled for her key, balancing the grocery bag on her knee until Kevin took it from her.

"What's that supposed to mean?"

She opened the heavy double doors and let him in. "I don't know, forget I said it." Erin sighed, leaning heavily against the mailboxes. "This is terrible, Kevin. I'm on edge, I don't know how to act, I don't know what to say. What do lovers do in Phase Two?"

"Sometimes they begin by saying that they're glad to see each other."

She pursed her lips and nodded. "That's it, I don't know whether I'm glad or not. I don't mean to hurt your feelings, it's me, not you. I mean it's me because of you." She closed her eyes and groaned. "Oh, God."

"And you think this is easy for me? I don't know what the rules are, either. I haven't been involved with a twenty-four-year-old since I was one. I don't want you to think I came into town tonight just to get you into bed." He turned from her with the case and the grocery bag and started up the stairs. "I do think it's possible for us to discuss this some place other than the foyer."

When they reached the apartment, Erin took the bag back and put it in the kitchen. Kevin looked around, commented on the fact that he hadn't been there since she'd joined the group in September and put his things in Nancy's room.

"I'm glad to see you," she said when he'd returned. "That *is* a good place to start. Now why don't you begin by telling me what you'd do if I were a thirty-seven-year-old who knew the rules."

"I'd fix her a drink and offer to help with dinner."

"Sounds good to me. I'll have a gin and tonic while I whip up some fettucine. It won't take long." When the water was on to boil and a salad had been tossed, they took their drinks to the couch by the open window. Kevin sipped and smiled.

Erin sipped and smiled and sighed. "How are the dogs and the kids and the bogs?"

"Fine, fine and fine." He cocked his head toward the window. "Debussy, how civilized."

"Chopin, I think."

He gave her a thoughtful look. "You've never been one to hesitate with your opinions. I knew this was how I'd find you, back to business at hand and ruling the roost."

Erin sipped and thought better of asking him what choice she had. She sat quietly, enjoying the physical reactions going on inside as she looked at him. What harm would it do her to reach over and touch his cheek, to brush her lips across his?

With a hiss the boiling water spilled from its pot as the steam drove the lid askew. Just as well, she thought as she jumped from the couch. Just as well. They ate at the table, toasting Chopin, twirling the pasta into the creamy sauce. When the pauses grew strained, one or the other of them made small talk. It was civilized and safe, and the ground was back beneath her feet.

With time to spare they walked to the Copley station and took the train to Kenmore Square with hundreds of other baseball fans. Erin held the overhead strap and when Kevin put his arm around her, she leaned into him, very much aware of how wonderful it felt. They sat in the bleachers and fed each other popcorn, screamed for Boston and moaned when the California Angels grabbed a temporary lead. Erin threw herself into the game; it gave her something else to concentrate on. The Red Sox managed to take the lead in the seventh inning, which they held until the Angels admitted defeat, in the bottom of the ninth. To celebrate, Erin and Kevin wandered with the crowd along Commonwealth Avenue and stopped into a watering hole populated more by the students and young professionals who lived in the neighborhood than the sports fans.

Erin sipped her beer and watched Kevin peruse the crowd. "Do this much?" he asked when they'd been served.

"Occasionally with friends. You're the one who looks uncomfortable," she said.

Kevin sighed. "I've got fifteen years on the next oldest person in here and that's the bartender."

"You're exaggerating," Erin replied. "There's only thirteen years between us."

"God," he muttered as he stared into his mug.

She had to admit it sounded formidable when spoken out loud. They left the air-conditioning for the stuffy bustle of the return trip. Marlborough Street was quiet under the gaslight. Somewhere a cat yowled as they climbed the stoop. "It seems years ago that I was too intimidated to ask you in for coffee that Sunday afternoon when you walked me back from Sky's."

"I'm not sure that woman still exists," Kevin replied.

Erin stepped up so she could look into his eyes. "Sexually, she doesn't. Don't wince just because you're responsible. Taking charge of my own emotions has been liberating; you've taught me to know myself. For example, I know tomorrow we'll go back to our separate lives and I've learned that that means you and I must go upstairs to separate beds."

Pain and slow, sad acknowledgment filtered through his features. It wasn't necessary to give him reasons and mentally she thanked him for not asking what they were. With his looks and track record, Kevin probably had enough experience to sense that she was dangerously close to falling in love with him.

The proposition would have been irrelevant anyway; Matt was sitting in the living room. They all stayed up another hour, Erin doing her best to be witty and impersonal. It was a relief when they agreed on bed and went to their respective rooms. It hadn't been a late night and the sound of the Branigan brothers laughing awoke her at seven in the morning. Matt and Kevin were at the table eating a full-course breakfast.

She appeared in front of them with her robe tastefully tied and her hair brushed. Kevin toasted her with his orange juice without so much as a glint in his eye. It shouldn't have depressed her as much as it did. "I'm going to drive Matt to the hospital and finally see where all the tuition's going," he said.

"Lovely." She pushed at her hair. When she'd returned to her room to dress they returned to the topic at hand, which, from what Erin could make out, was her shining future with Harvard's teaching hospitals.

Goodbyes consisted of thank-yous for the baseball game, a fraternal kiss and the same damnable ache in her breastbone. At the hospital she accepted a dinner offer from an intern and suggested a Mexican restaurant since she couldn't digest spicy food. She was looking forward to a case of heartburn that didn't spring from emotional causes.

Sunday night Erin sat in the cafeteria making patterns in her Styrofoam coffee cup with the stir rod only minutes from her next childbirth class. Three days since the ball game. Three crummy days without a word from the man who made mad, passionate love as easily as he drove a car. What did she expect? Surely not a platonic, long-distance relationship with a thirty-seven-year-old. The Kevin Branigans of this world didn't operate that way, which Matthew Branigan had made perfectly clear before she'd even set foot in Millbrook.

Eleven

———

When she was through analyzing Kevin, she turned to herself. Congratulations should have been in order. Only perceptive, mature women who knew themselves as well as she did would still be standing after a week as intense as hers had been at the bogs. After all, could she really handle a romance of that magnitude at this distance? She wasn't ready and if Kevin had suggested it, she would have backed down. At any rate, it was painful to recall that Kevin hadn't suggested it.

Monday was her day off and she slept late. As June ended, the fickle New England summer arrived in earnest. She dressed in a shift and pinned up her hair. Although she had ample invitations to area beaches and Cape Cod summer rentals, she wasn't eligible for a full-fledged vacation until September. She was contemplating a stroll through Quincy Market when there was a rap at the door. She pulled open the door, expecting to find one of her neighbors who shared the converted town house. Kevin stood on the landing, a niece holding each of his hands.

"Good morning, you remember Kate and Suzanne."

Erin gave a halfhearted attempt to hide her joy. "I do. You're the one I'm not sure I remember. How'd you get in?"

"Kevin Branigan, cranberry baron, at your service. The piano player on the fourth floor was coming in with groceries and sheet music. I complimented her on the Chopin and I guess she decided that a man with two kids in tow and an ear for the classics wouldn't be up to anything suspicious."

"I could have told her differently. What *are* you doing here?"

"We're going to take you on the Swan Boats," Kate replied.

"Uncle Kevin says we have to be tourists because it's the season," Suzanne added.

Erin looked at Kevin, who shrugged. "You got me thinking about what a family tradition it was. It's time the next generation had a chance. We took a chance you'd join us. I'll even throw in a sundae at Bailey's."

The rush of her pulse when she looked into his eyes was as pleasant as the thought of ice cream and every bit as tempting. The four of them set out on foot for the walk to the Public Garden at the head of Marlborough Street. Kate's feet gave out on the way and Kevin hoisted her onto his shoulders where she giggled and hugged his forehead as they made their way into the garden. They stopped on the footbridge and watched the boats that had glided for generations over the pond. At the stern a teenager foot-paddled the boat from his seat on the back of an artificial swan, while tourists sat on the half-dozen benches in front of him.

Suzanne was the first to become restless, tugging at Kevin and trying to hurry him along.

"Your Uncle Matt nearly fell in the last time I was here," Kevin admonished. "Watch your step and stay in line." He lifted Kate off his shoulders and she joined her sister, precariously close to the water's edge.

Erin made idle conversation as Kevin grew pensive and she finally left him to his thoughts as he watched his nieces. When it was their turn to board, they put the girls together on the outside, next to the water. "Thank you for including me," Erin said quietly as they were paddled over the water.

Kevin nodded. "As the reputed head of the family, I figured it was up to me to get this tradition going again. It's good for their little souls."

Erin was about to reply as he opened his hand across his eyes and squeezed his temples. Without a word she took his free hand in both of hers and held it, looking, as he was, up into the thick green canopy of treetops. When the moment passed, Kevin freed his hand. "I didn't think it would be so tough."

"Memories have a way of intruding no matter what you try to do to avoid them," she replied.

They docked amid the next passengers and paused once they were back on land to watch a mallard and her serpentine line of ducklings. From there Erin and Kevin made their way across Boston Common with the girls scampering along. "They remind me of Max and Domino," Erin remarked as they went.

At the bustle of Park Street Station, Kevin lifted Kate again while Erin took Suzanne's hand. They paused to watch a banjo-playing street musician and then crossed the street to the landmark ice-cream parlor. "Will you be all right in here?" Erin asked as he held the door.

Kevin nodded. "Cranberry growers are as tough as their crop."

"Or else they think they are," she said as she passed him.

In addition to the ice cream, Bailey's offered nostalgia that hit Erin, too. As she looked at the gleaming brass and polished marble, it was easy to imagine Kate Branigan and her boys perched at the fountain or sitting around one of the little tables. She stole a glance at Kevin as he ordered for the girls, but his face was like a mask. What she read was the effort at composure and high spirits.

Window-shopping proved to be the diversion they both needed. They lost themselves in the displays in Filene's and Jordan Marsh, bought small, tacky trinkets on Washington Street for the girls and when their feet gave out, piled into a taxi for the return to the town house.

The apartment was as they'd left it, with the exception of a note from Matt. He wrote that he'd been home to shower and was spending the night in the medical school dormitory in order to join an obstetrical study group. Erin arched her eyebrows and looked at Kevin. "Your brother's quite taken with this rotation. I think he's discovered it's a lot more lively than gastrointestinal maladies." Entirely different patient profile, too, she added to herself.

"Do you think he'll change his specialty?" Kevin asked.

"He's got another year before his residency. You Branigans are a pragmatic bunch; I'm sure he'll weigh all the pros and cons."

"I'm hungry," Kate declared.

Kevin patted her head. "We'll get something on the way home. Hang on a minute, sweetheart."

Suzanne looked up at Erin. "Couldn't we have a sleepover here? We could all help cook . . ."

Erin looked at Kevin. "I've got the room and you'll avoid the rush hour. Matt's got plenty of whatever you need and I can wash out the girls' things."

Over the begging, pleading and tugging at his pants, Kevin acquiesced. "After we call your mommy. If she says yes we'll stay."

Anne's yes was enthusiastic, adding that Sean had come off a forty-eight-hour shift and that she'd love the chance to be alone with him. It was all settled in fifteen minutes.

The youngsters explored the bedrooms while Erin explored her feelings. She watched Kevin light the hibachi on the fire escape while she made hamburger patties and put together a salad. It gave the illusion of domestic bliss. Bizarre, she thought. They'd never had what the rest of the world considered a proper date.

They ate on a tablecloth spread on the living-room floor and pretended they were in an enchanted forest. Erin filled the evening with camp songs and whimsy, catching Kevin's glance occasionally as he studied the three of them. She bathed the girls while he did the dishes and then, much to their delight, let them pick from her lingerie. Kate made an impromptu nightgown from a camisole tied across the shoulder blades with a shoelace, while Suzanne slithered into a slip that fell below her knees. If Kevin recognized either item, he had the good sense to keep it to himself. After washing out the girls' ice-cream-covered clothing, Erin and Kevin made up a story for each in lieu of any children's books and tucked them into Nancy's bed. After prayers and wet kisses they giggled for five minutes and fell soundly asleep.

"Angels," Erin murmured as Kevin turned on the television.

"They do have a way about them," he sighed.

The children's presence had been a buffer and without them silence replaced their chatter. "How about a drink? I've got some gin and cranberry juice or tonic," Erin offered, as much to make conversation as to give herself something to concentrate on.

"Fine with me. Good idea," Kevin replied.

She made two Cape Codders and added a twist of lime. Kevin took one as he thumbed through the *New England Journal of Medicine*. Summer television reruns were a poor substitute for the way previous evenings had been spent— poor but safe. Erin would have loved to talk about the episode on the Swan Boats, or the anguish in Bailey's, but feelings that close to the bone were for Kevin to mention. Even as she prayed he would, she could feel him retreat.

"This is awful!" he exclaimed suddenly.

She blanched. "Cranberry juice and gin? I thought in your line of work..."

"Not the drink, the situation. I don't know what in blue blazes to do with you, Erin." He got up from the couch. "Look at me, wandering around your apartment muttering to myself. Does she want me to make a pass at her? Will she be insulted? Is everything over? Shall I keep it light like the last visit?" He looked down at her and jammed his hands into his pockets, rattling car keys. "I'm sure I've been in this situation before, but I'll be damned if I can remember when. I know for a fact I've never felt the need to drag two toddlers along to keep me out of trouble."

Erin pursed her lips as she watched him, marveling at the leaping of her heart. "Why don't you start by sitting back down and finishing your drink?" she said, patting the cushion.

He did and when he'd taken a long swallow, he put his head back. "I fully agree with your feelings, Erin: separate lives, separate beds. It's been too much, too fast for you. I'll always blame myself for that, for the way you look at me with those big brown eyes."

"What way is that?" she managed.

"There's a sadness that wasn't there before. You've replaced all that wonder with knowledge."

"Part of that knowledge is knowing myself, Kevin. If there's sadness it's because, even with all your experience, you hold emotion back. Heaven knows I don't mean sex. I mean what happened to you this afternoon at the Swan Boats. You'd do well to look less closely at me and more closely at yourself." Erin got up and turned off the television neither of them was watching, plunging the room, again, into expectant silence.

When Kevin remained quiet, she tiptoed to the girls' room, checked on them and closed the door. "Your chaperons are sound asleep," she whispered as she turned back around. He was standing behind her, his chest rising and falling in steady, shallow movements. "You shouldn't have come and gotten me this morning, Kevin. You shouldn't have made me part of that family tradition as if you had to prove there was more to us than a week of fun and games." She started past him but he touched her shoulder and left his open hand along the side of her neck.

"Erin, I came to apologize, but I can't get within three feet of you without losing every damned ounce of common sense I've ever possessed." He closed his fingers and she stepped forward, pushing away the foreboding.

"Was this to be the last time?" she asked.

He closed his eyes as he bent his arms to enfold her. "No. The last time was in Millbrook. I had some crazy idea that we could be friends, family . . . the way we were before. The way you are with Matt."

Erin tried desperately to think, to clear her head and give him nice, pragmatic reasons why they could be. Against her breasts, his chest heaved, his heart thundered in time to hers. Rational thought was useless. "Before? There was nothing before," she whispered. Nothing but an even-keeled existence free of the torture of yearning and uncertainty. The desire with which she was learning to live widened, not gradually, but with a sudden yawning tear inside. She touched him as if he were an addiction, fighting the urge to cling. Never again, she told herself, but once more, just this one last time.

"I'll go," he moaned as her hands trembled. "I swear I never meant..." But he'd already slid his hands over her back, thumbs wide along her ribs, to rest and cup her bottom. She swayed gently and found the magic spot at the base of his spine.

She was up in his arms and behind her closed, locked, bedroom door without another word, without another apology. For the moment she left behind all but the vivid memory of what they'd been and the need to have it again. If Erin's physical desire was based on anything deeper than this moment's urgency, she left that behind, as well.

The troubled, pensive man, bent on making sense of everything was gone with a curse. Kevin threw off his clothes and roughly worked Erin from hers. "To have this with you, love, night after night and then... nothing. I look at those woods where we were, remember the pine needles in my bed... Erin, one last time, please..."

They fell onto the mattress and clung to each other, abandoning everything but their mutual need to satisfy. Immediately intimate, they prepared for what they knew lay moments ahead, for what they'd already shared so many times. As if he had to memorize every curve, Kevin kissed and touched her skin, playing games she begged for as he traveled the length of her. Kevin's skin was hot to her touch, hotter still when he spoke her name with a groan and positioned her under him. In the moments that followed they made sweet, silent love, first one, then the other, then both torn apart and made whole.

Kevin kissed her fingertips as he lay beside her, savoring the last of the euphoria. "There's an incredibly beautiful chemistry between us."

"More of a problem than a solution," she replied.

Kevin sighed. "You give yourself so completely, it scares the life out of me. I don't want to be responsible for the hurt; I never want you to know that pain. I've been drunk with desire for you, Erin, there's no other way to put it. It's a very selfish feeling. You're right," he reiterated, "you're right to want to slow this down. The hell of it is, it's going to take both of us to make it work."

"And that's what you want, too?"

Kevin looked at her and nodded. "It's what has to be. If you were my age, if you were even four or five years older, things might be different. I might not worry."

An ache that began in Erin's throat radiated up behind her eyes and made her blink against the sting. "I really can't help how old I am."

"No, but I can help what I'm doing to you," Kevin said.

"I hate it when cranberry growers get all noble and self-sacrificing."

"Believe me, this isn't a role I'm used to. You started it, love, with your wisdom after the baseball game. If we're living separate lives, then this can't go on. It's important for you to open yourself to the life you're living. You have a fabulous career, a world in medicine. You belong out there rubbing up against the challenge and the minds of the people you work with."

"And rubbing up against anything else?"

Kevin shifted and was quiet for a moment. "It will happen, Erin. I'm not suggesting that you jump into bed, but I know you. As long as you and I are physically involved, you'll cut yourself off from what's been important, what's been the focus of your life until now. The things you love me for now, you'll hate me for later. You'll resent me for taking that away; it would break your heart and that would break mine."

Erin held his hand against her breast and nodded. "We don't seem to be able to separate things, hard as we try." She forced the sob down into her chest. "I didn't mean what I said before about not being friends. I'd like to try, I don't want to lose that."

"Neither do I," he whispered. "Just keep an open mind, get your feet back on the ground."

"Kevin, you'll go back to other friends, too, of course?"

He was quiet, as if waiting for the hurt to settle in both of them. "That isn't why I brought this up."

"But it would be an option—for both of us."

"Yes, it might."

Her eyes burned and her throat was closed and she damned nobility and common sense as he gathered his clothes. "I would have said all this if you hadn't," she managed.

"I know." He stood above her and stroked her hair before pulling up the sheet. "I'll see you in the morning."

"You're right, Kevin. I've loved you because you're compassionate and thoughtful and far more experienced at this, and now I hate you for it."

Twelve

Like a long-suffering married couple in the midst of an argument, Erin and Kevin focused on the children in the morning. They were determined to rise above the less than bright atmosphere in the apartment.

Erin was due at the hospital, the weather was threatening and Kevin was hurrying the girls through their breakfast. "One stop on the way home, the Aquarium or the Children's museum?"

"Fish," Kate said.

"Museum," replied her sister.

"They're young, let them experience both," Erin said to Kevin, ignoring the sharp turn of his head. She was in her uniform, hair up, anxious to have them gone.

At the front door, she knelt and hugged the girls and stood back up to look at Kevin. "The engagement party's in two weeks," he said. "There's room for you at the house and there'll be plenty of chaperons."

"I know. I'll see how things are by then." Kevin and the girls left as the rain started and Erin went to the hospital. She proceeded to throw herself into her work. July and August were months notoriously empty of extra hands, and Erin was needed.

Her bleary-eyed roommate noticed, as well. "You're leaving *me* notes, now," Matt said at breakfast. "All these extra hours at the hospital and I should suspect you of lusting after a doctor, but your mood's too lousy for it to be love."

Erin sipped her orange juice. "You're so hyped up on obstetrics, you think a normal disposition is depression, Harvard."

He laughed. "Maybe you're right. I had no idea I'd take to it. It's changing my mind about my residency, Erin. I've been thinking about Women and Children's Hospital."

"You'll never have the free time you'd get in Gastro."

He nodded thoughtfully. "Yes, but it's life instead of death."

"Women and their problems, too."

Matt frowned and studied her. "You *are* down. Work?"

"Frustrated by my lack of authority, I guess. I had so much freedom in Millbrook, so much chance to use my own administrative skills. I'm basically a bossy person. I think I was born to give orders," she replied with a sigh.

"It's not enough to stand with a laboring patient and yell, 'push'?"

Erin laughed. "Most of the time it is, but there are moments when I think I'd rather push papers. I don't know, Kevin, I'm just discontent at the moment."

"You must be," Matt replied, "you just called me Kevin."

"Now, there's a slip of the tongue."

Matt studied her. "Was it? You two have been keeping close quarters lately. The morning I drove him to the hospital, all we talked about was you."

"How decidedly dull."

"Erin, don't go getting some ridiculous crush on him. You could never handle it. He's way out of your league." Matt's expression darkened. "Has he put pressure on you?"

"Matthew, really. Your brother's a perfect gentleman and I'm hardly his type," she replied truthfully. Determined to drop the subject, she started up on the cases she'd seen recently, which lasted until she left for the hospital.

Matt seemed to have forgotten their conversation when they caught up with each other after dinner. Erin announced that she was going for a walk in what daylight remained and Matt decided to go along. They walked off in the direction of the Esplanade along the Charles River where the Boston Pops were giving their open-air concert in the Hatch Shell.

On the footbridge over Storrow Drive, they stopped and watched the crowd as it gathered and when Matt recognized some friends, he hurried her along to the park. Fifteen minutes later Erin was sitting on a blanket, drinking white wine with three of Matt's classmates, including a Californian named Greg Cooper. Though he was a year her senior, he seemed young, and quite green. Still, they salvaged the evening with good conversation and a nightcap in a Newbury Street pub. Matt had long since returned home when Greg meandered back with her along Dartmouth Street. He left her at her stoop with a smile and a promise to call. She said she'd like that and she tried to mean it.

The following day she argued twice with a physician who had half the knowledge of her patient's personality than she did and once with the head nurse over a teenager in labor. It was nothing out of the ordinary, but she was in no mood to apologize for her opinions. She went home between her shift and her evening childbirth class in the hopes that she'd have two hours to herself.

The apartment smelled of garlic bread and minestrone soup. "You again," Matt called from the kitchen. "How nice."

She came up behind him and accepted his offered glass of jug wine. "Cheers."

"Same to you. Greg called and Sky did, too. She's having a cookout and parade party on the Fourth of July. You haven't lived till you've watched them march in Millbrook. Come with me. Of course the parade goes right past Schuyler House."

"I don't know."

"Erin, if this funk has anything to do with my brother..."

"I have an invitation to Marblehead for the Fourth," she lied. "Heavens, you're more obsessed with Kevin than I am," she snapped. When she realized what had slipped out of her mouth, she took refuge in her room and changed her clothes. Matt was standing on the other side of the door when she opened it.

"Run that past me again, the part about obsessed," he said.

She tried to sidestep past him. "It was a slip of the tongue."

"Yet another. This one sounded Freudian."

"Matthew, I've seen about ten times as much of your oldest brother as I have of you in the past month. Okay, I was infatuated. Nothing more."

"So he *did* pressure you!"

"You're being ridiculous! Whatever feelings there might have been were mutual."

Matt had already begun to steam and he followed her into the living room at her heels. "Don't try to stick up for him.

Insinuating that you gave him encouragement is crazy. I live with you, I double date with you. Believe me, I'd know if you were giving off those kinds of vibes.''

Erin started to laugh. "I think that was meant as a compliment. Matt, will you stop mothering me?"

"If you've been fooling around with Kevin Branigan, you need a whole lot more than mothering."

"Look, everything is under control. I'll go to Sky's on the Fourth. You come with me and you'll see there's nothing destructive going on between your treacherous oldest brother and your sweet, innocent roommate. Now if you don't mind, I'd like to stop fighting long enough to eat." Her intentions for the holiday slipped out as innocently as the word *obsession*, but Millbrook was, after all, where she wanted to be and if Kevin couldn't handle it, he could watch the parade from the fire station.

Kevin didn't watch from across the street. He stood with the rest of the family and guests on the sidewalk against Sky's iron fence. He'd been on the lawn when Matt arrived with Erin and Greg. When she introduced one to the other, Erin said, "I thought a jaded medical student from California should see what a real old-fashioned Fourth of July looks like in New England. Kevin, this is Greg Cooper. Greg, Kevin Branigan, head of the clan." They shook hands and then Greg draped his arm back over her shoulder.

"Welcome to Millbrook," Kevin offered.

"Great to be here. Erin was telling me on the Esplanade the other night that Matt's family is into cranberries. Just fascinating."

"Can be. Any agriculture in your California background?"

Greg tossed his blond hair. "Medicine, actually, and oil. My father's chief of OB/GYN at L.A. Hospital. Oil's on my mother's side."

"Well, I guess you and Erin have a lot in common, through your father's side of the family, anyway."

"Yes, we do," he replied.

Kevin looked out over Sky's guests, the majority related to him. "Enjoy the parade, you two. Erin, make sure he gets a tour of the house." He left them with a final handshake and smile, wandering off in the direction of the ice chest. It seemed to Erin that the least he could have done was to look envious or jealous; melancholy would have helped. She sighed.

There were two grills going and picnic fare for everyone. Greg made easy conversation with everyone he was introduced to and at two he and Erin assembled with the others at the iron fence. Neighbors had lined the sidewalk with miniature American flags that fluttered in the light breeze as the group turned in the direction of Pilgrim Street.

There were three bands from area high schools and minutemen from the Ancient and Honorable Militia. Brass blared, muskets were fired. Sean stood with his daughters, who clapped and screamed with glee as the fire trucks paused and aimed their hoses at the common. Arcs of water shot into the air, leaving rainbows in the mist, then with a blast from their sirens, the trucks moved down the street. As the parade quieted, Erin's attention was diverted by Ryan's and Kevin's raised voices. Their backs were turned as they stood looking at the carriage barn, still in the process of being painted by Ryan's Police League teenagers. Ryan was defending the time away from the bogs; Kevin was complaining about the diversion.

As clowns on unicycles passed, the brothers lowered their voices in a truce. "Worse than ten-year-olds," Sky muttered from her spot next to Erin. "Ryan's a maverick, and he always will be. Kevin's been much better lately about it but this week..." She shook her head as they applauded the clowns' antics. "He's been a complete bear, snapping at everybody."

"I suppose he's under pressure to finish the barn and the workshops," Erin offered.

"The barn's been finished for days. This is vacation time. If they don't relax a little now, come September when the harvest gets close, I may exit permanently to Beacon Hill. Ryan's only trying to finish the carriage barn and help the painters with the last bedroom because my family's coming. Kevin seems to forget the stress his brother's under from having his fiancée be a Schuyler." Sky sighed. "There's a thorn in Kevin's paw for some reason and his wounded lion routine is tough on everyone. My family's about to descend on Ryan and he needs his brother's support, not his criticism."

Erin shook her head. "Maybe there's a lot on Kevin's mind. Maybe underneath it all he's jealous of Ryan's happiness with you."

"Not a chance. He's got Ryan out of the house. Kevin's life is exactly the way he wants it—King of the Heap, Head of the Family—and now all the privacy he could ask for. He'll be the first to tell you that he's living his life on his own terms."

"And I'll be the second," Erin added.

Sky laughed. "Yes, I guess you had your own first-hand look."

The women stopped to admire the homemade floats as they passed. Sky changed the subject to the clinic. "Women's Services begins tomorrow. The board decided to phase in the parenting courses in the fall so they'll have time to target the patient population. It's going to be quite a boon to this area when everything's in full swing. I'm taking some time off to get my own life in order, but I'll miss it."

"Everybody else have vacation plans?" Erin asked.

"After the engagement party, Sean and Drew are taking their families down east for most of August, I think. They've rented a house near Rockland, Maine. I'm trying to get Ryan to my brother Jake's place on Nantucket."

"And where's the King of the Hill off to?" Erin asked casually.

"He hasn't said, but if I know him, he'll stay put and contemplate the solitude with the dogs. He doesn't like the property deserted; I know he'd rather not have everyone gone at once."

"Solitude becomes him," Erin said.

"He likes to think so."

They turned back to the parade, cheering wildly for the final float and the straggling clowns, limp from the long hours in the heat. Greg, Erin noticed, was enjoying himself thoroughly, as comfortable in her company as Jody's and Matt's. If Kevin threw her any furtive glances or regretful sighs, she missed them. She was disgusted with herself for dwelling on it as if she'd expected him to drag her into the lilac hedge with confessions that he'd been a fool to have given her up. Erin came close to patting Ryan's arm and telling him she knew just how he felt. Kevin knew what was best for the Branigans and he'd wrapped her in that same fraternal guidance.

At three o'clock, with everyone in the back garden involved in games or conversation, Greg reminded Erin that he had a five o'clock call at the hospital. They thanked Ryan and Sky together and while Greg made small talk about Sky's family mansion on Beacon Hill, Erin looked at the ex-police officer. "Kevin's giving you a hard time, I gather."

Ryan shrugged. "Nothing out of the ordinary except a bizarre accusation that I've neglected my goddaughters by not taking them on the Swan Boats. Swan Boats! I'm lucky if I can meet the hundred other things on his list. Sorry, Erin, I didn't mean to unload this on you. It'll blow over, it always does." He hugged her and added the anticipation of seeing her at the engagement party.

From there she went in search of Matt to tell him Greg was waiting. After searching the familiar faces on the lawn, she went around the house to the deserted street side and finally through the screen door into the front hall. She stopped in her tracks in the wide foyer outside the door to Sky's library as two painfully familiar voices lost what little composure they'd had.

"Calm down, damn it! I've apologized. I feel lousy about it, but you're accusing me of ridiculous things," Kevin was saying.

"Did you honestly think you could take her away from men like Greg Cooper? What was this, the ultimate challenge? She doesn't mean a thing to you." Matt's voice lowered in an angry growl. "This is low, Kevin, even for you."

"I never intended to take her away from anyone. Give Erin some credit, will you? She's a wonderful person, we had a great week."

Erin's heart froze and then slammed erratically under her ribs, but she didn't move. However, from the sounds of it, furniture in the library did. "How could you take advantage of her? She came down here to work. Kevin, I thought she'd have a change of scene, get out of the city, enjoy herself."

"She did."

Heavy footsteps made Erin jump back, but they stopped as though one brother had held the other at bay. "Matthew, listen to me," Kevin pleaded with an affectionate laugh. "I don't know how I managed to instill so much chivalry in you, but your roommate doesn't need it. I guess sooner or later a woman was bound to foul things up between one or another of us. Remember when Holly came? You accused me of falling in love with her instead of running her out of town on a rail. Trust me, little brother, I know a few things about adult relationships." Erin caught the strain as he tried to keep things light.

"That's enough of your smug jokes, Kevin. This is Erin we're talking about." Matt seemed to be pushing a chair aside.

When Kevin responded the lilt was gone from his voice. "Long after Erin O'Connor is out of your life *and* mine, we'll still be family. Don't let something this trivial come between us. I've apologized, it was a mistake, it's *over*, Matt."

There was an audible intake of breath. "How could the others stand by? Ryan, Drew and Sean have no idea, do they? Not even Jody. He was going to take her out while she was here. Did you lie to all of them?"

"No," Kevin said evenly. "There were no lies. It was something private between Erin and me, Matt, and it's *finished*. She's a wonderful, loving person. She's a woman, too, not made of porcelain. She's flesh and blood with her own desires..."

The sentence came to a thundering halt with a loud thud. Erin found her voice as she ran through the doorway. "That's enough out of both of you!"

Kevin was sprawled over the arm of the chesterfield couch, grimacing, his open hand against his jaw. Blood trickled against his lower lip. Matt stood next to him, cradling a limp right fist in his left hand, blowing on his knuckles.

"Of all the lame-brained, idiotic, chauvinistic things to do! Matthew Branigan, I am perfectly capable of taking care of myself and that includes choosing whom to be intimate with. If I acted with an appalling lack of judgment the first time around, I'm to blame. If you have any thought whatsoever of a career ministering to the female gender, then you had better learn something more than how they're put together physically."

She turned her attention to Kevin, whose painful half-grin rapidly disappeared. "And as for you. You may know plenty about a woman's emotions, Kevin Branigan, but you haven't a clue as to what to do with your own. Ryan doesn't need to be the butt of your frustration just because you got all choked up on the Swan Boats and can't bear to share your grief any more than you can share your love. I haven't come between you and your brother, I've come between you and your facade."

Their expressions grew incredulous and with a toss of her hair, she thrust a tissue at Kevin. "Your lip's split and it's my professional medical opinion that your jaw needs ice. Get yourself into the kitchen. Sky has enough on her mind without having to worry about getting your blood out of her carpet. Matt, you might as well follow him and wrap your hand in ice, too. Greg can drive or I will. If you think it needs an X ray, you can check in with your buddies in Radiology when we drop Greg at the hospital. You have rounds tomorrow and if it's immobile, Dr. Bauer's going to be just about as impressed with your behavior as I am. The next time I need a roommate, she'll be female, and the next time I fall in love, you can be certain, he'll be an only child."

Erin led the way from the room, through the butler's pantry to the kitchen, where the brothers rifled the drawers for plastic bags and dish towels and got ice from the freezer. She gave them both a final sigh. "Matt, I'll see you at the car. If you two are as decent and high-minded as you think you are, I hope you'll come up with a whopper of an explanation for all this. I'd like to go back to Boston without being the topic of a lot of conjecture and gossip. You're right, Kevin, soon I will be out of your lives and I'd like to think there won't be an Erin O'Connor Episode tossed around the Branigan living rooms.'' She marched from the room oblivious to the anguish in both brothers' eyes.

Thirteen

Matt told Greg that he'd been arguing with Kevin, that they'd both been stupid but that Kevin deserved the slug. Erin glared into the back seat where Matt sat nursing his swollen knuckles and they joined the Cape traffic winding its way north to Boston.

At the physicians' entrance to the hospital, Greg idled Matt's car and gave Erin a kiss. "Great day. I'll keep in touch, though my schedule's no better than his."

"I'd like that," Erin replied, moving into the driver's seat. Matt pronounced his hand healing and she drove back to Marlborough Street. Ten minutes later, with the car parked in the alley, she handed Matt his keys. "I hope you're not going to slug Gregory Cooper because he kissed me just now. I might let him do it again, if the mood strikes."

Matt unlocked the building with his good hand. "I'm glad you're treating this so lightly, because I'm too busy to pick up the pieces and Nancy's gone till fall. I went overboard, I admit it, but you fell in love with him, damn it, and that's what I was afraid of."

"What ever gave you that idea? It was just infatuation on both our parts."

"Erin, you're knocking yourself out to have me believe that, but love is what you called it."

"I didn't," she protested.

Matt stopped on the third-floor landing and looked at her. "In the past week you've called me *Kevin*, referred to the fling as an obsession and in Sky's library, not two hours ago, you told us the next time you fall in love, it'll be with an only child. I might add that it's written all over your face. As a fledgling physician, I should have recognized the symptoms."

Erin pushed past him and resumed the climb. "If I used the word *love*, it was in the heat of the moment. I was upset! You could have knocked his teeth out, not to mention the injury to your hand. Never mind, Kevin spoke for both of us. It's over. It was just one of those crazy things, bound to happen sooner or later."

"Not with my brother," Matt muttered.

Erin unlocked their apartment and closed her eyes against the hot blast of lifeless air. "Never mind, Harvard. He's too old for me, too devoted to his independence, too removed from my life and work here. I'm holding out for the chief of Neurosurgery."

"Far more appropriate."

"I thought you'd think so."

In the two weeks that followed, Erin had dinner with Greg and spent a balmy July afternoon with him playing tennis. He was delightful company and no more interested in a long-term relationship than she was. He also accepted her gentle *no* when he pressed for more than a nightcap. She loved the pace and flavor of Boston in the summer and made the most of her time off.

Having taken Kevin's advice to heart, it was as if she carried him there, as well. He had opened the world to her, though they had barely left Millbrook. He would be proud of her, she knew. How ironic that she longed to share so much of her new life with him, to tell him how right he'd been. Though he was never completely off her mind, she knew there'd be no more surprise visits. That knowledge settled her some. She moved forward as the physical ache subsided.

The engagement party at the Millbrook Country Club was the last Saturday night in July. Buoyed by her newly returned equilibrium, Erin packed for the night in the house she'd share not only with Kevin, but Ryan, Matt and Jody. Because of their work schedules, she and her roommate dressed for the formal affair in Boston and planned to drive directly to the dinner-dance at seven.

"The Schuylers are calling the shots tonight," Matt mumbled as Erin adjusted the tie to his tuxedo before they left. "I hate these things."

Erin smoothed a lapel. "A man never looks handsomer. Besides, with all of you dressed to the nines, there's less chance of rowdy behavior. Can I trust you?" she teased.

He narrowed his eyes. "Can I trust *you*?"

"I'm dressed for trusting, too." She twirled for him, her black silk sheath widening with the motion and falling back to drape her thighs. Her hair fell in masses of reddish waves across her bare shoulders. She wore a single strand of pearls at her throat and, unlike Anne's bathing suit, the bodice of her dress had been tailored to fit. Her breasts molded to the fabric properly, a hint of cleavage rising from the demure design. It would have been strapless except for the narrow bands of silk that tied on each shoulder.

"That's debatable," Matt replied as she finished spinning.

Erin grew serious. "Matt, you love me like a sister. Will you accept me as a woman who knows what she's doing? I think these past weeks have proven to you that I'm fully in charge of my own life, and my own feelings. You'll ruin my evening if I have to fret about you."

"You're talking as though you've got something up your noticeably absent sleeve."

"I don't, honestly. I want to go to the party and have a wonderful time."

He picked up their bags and motioned for the door. "Then let's see that you do."

It was cooler in the country, but still close to eighty degrees when Matt handed the valet his car keys. "Did you know this is how Sky and Ryan met? She came here for a deb party and he was parking cars, summer job. Handed him the keys to that old Mercedes—which was brand-new at the time—and that was it."

"Until the Schuylers and Kevin stepped in."

"It was a temporary separation." He shot her a studied expression. "Don't go getting any ideas."

Erin took his arm and pushed Matt in the direction of the party. "Could we just go and enjoy ourselves, please?"

The reception was being held on the brick patio at the end of the imposing building. Japanese lanterns and landscape lights had been strung in the maple branches in a canopy effect. Beyond the area designated for receiving the guests were shadowed boxwood gardens and a tent large enough to accommodate a dance floor and the buffet supper.

A string quartet was playing as Erin and Matt arrived. There was no receiving line, but as hostess, Sarah Schuyler, the widowed head of the family, and John Schuyler III, known as Jake, Sky's brother and the host, greeted Sky's friends and future in-laws. Kevin, as head of the Branigan family, stood with the engaged couple. As Erin stepped from the shadows onto the patio, she saw Kevin's head turn and felt the warmth of his glance as he watched her introduce herself and Matt to Sky's family.

Erin lingered with the older woman and complimented her on the Beacon Hill house. She mentioned her connection to Sky and then turned to Jake and talked Manhattan versus Boston. She hugged Sky, got a kiss from Ryan and then moved in a slow pivot to drink in the full effect of the man waiting beside his middle brother. She was unprepared for the rush of her pulse, but the color was in his cheeks also. With the exception of New Year's Eve, she'd never seen him in any but casual clothes. He stood now in his dinner jacket, pleated dress shirt, cummerbund and black tie, not unlike every other man in attendance, except that he was not any other man.

A flush had settled over his cheekbones and his blue eyes were bright with affection. It wasn't desire or excitement, there was too much contentment in the glance for those. As Erin smiled up at him it seemed to her that he had just sighed, some mental question answered.

"Hello, Kevin," she said as they took each other's hands. Sky, Ryan, Jake and Matt were watching. "Be careful when you shake your brother's hand," she added. "His knuckles are still tender." She put the four pads of her fingertips against the side of his face but didn't press. "I suspect your jaw is, too, although I don't see any signs of swelling."

He shook his head, the color deepening over the bridge of his nose. "Miss O'Connor, unless you've changed your mind about being the subject of conjecture, I suggest you lower your voice and choose another subject for small talk."

Erin patted his arm in mute agreement as she made room for Matt and the following guests to say hello. "As usual, your advice is right on the mark. I'll go find Drew and Holly and give you and your brother a chance to make up." She was about to add that she wanted no Branigan feuds on her account, but looked at those within earshot and thought better of it. Nevertheless, she was in a buoyant, devilish mood, her emotional upheaval under control. These moments were proof enough.

She walked from him aware that he was still watching and her spine tingled from the top under her tangle of hair to the base under the slip of silk. It might prove to be a long night. Erin found the twins and their wives, sipped champagne being passed in tulip glasses on silver trays and discussed children's sleep patterns. It relieved the tingling.

She was on her second glass when Jake raised his and quieted the guests. He stood with his mother and wife and some cousins and looked at his older sister. "On behalf of my family, I'd like to welcome all of you tonight. This is a match that must have been made in heaven because everybody on earth did their darnedest to break it up the first time around. I was at camp the summer Ryan and Sky dated and by the time I got home, Sky had been whisked off to Europe. From what I understand, Ryan had his own Grand Tour with Uncle Sam. Mother was still clutching the draperies and Kevin, who was head of the Branigans even then, got his first gray hairs at twenty-four."

When the laughter died down, he pulled a dog-eared postcard from his pocket and waved it just out of Sky's reach. "I doubt that she remembers this," he continued, "but my sister sent me a postcard from Vienna. It's my engagement present to Ryan." He cleared his throat for the delivery.

"Dear Jake,
In case you're hanging around the pool or the courts at

the club, keep your eye on the guy who rides the mower and tends the greens. He's Ryan Branigan and he's the reason I'm over here studying a bunch of dead guys' music. His brother Kevin and Mom and Dad planned this whole stupid thing to separate us. I've practically been kidnapped. Life can be gross when you love somebody and they think you're too young. You're not the only one I miss.

Love, Janey.

P.S. Beethoven's not so bad.''

As he finished, Jake grinned, kissed his sister and handed the card to Ryan. The guests cheered and Erin fought the lump in her throat. ''That was written fourteen years ago next month, and I'd like to propose a toast to my sister and her wisdom. I'm sorry my father's not here, but I know my mother shares my joy,'' Jake finished as Sarah Schuyler stepped forward.

She raised her glass to Kevin and winked. ''It's about time you and I admit defeat. May we all drink to the health and the love and the foresight of my daughter and my future son-in-law, Ryan.''

The old sting was back in Erin's eyes, but then half the assembled friends were dabbing at their lashes and sniffing into cocktail napkins. As Erin watched, Kevin kissed Sky and shared some private witticism. He turned to his family and to hers; they all deferred to him. It had been seven months since Erin had watched him across a room that first time. She had marvelled then, as she did now, at the ease with which he brought people together. What emotions had transpired since then! There had been awe, certainly, and respect, desire, frustration, even some anger. Compassion had played a part, empathy, too.

Now she watched him laugh at something Jake said and thought, I can make him laugh. I know what brings him to tears. I know what he wants in a woman and what he feels as a man. Because of Kevin Branigan, she wasn't the same person as the innocent who'd stood aside on New Year's Eve. He'd added a dimension to her personality that went far beyond her physical maturity. He'd helped her experience life at its richest and she brought it to all subsequent relationships. She was a better nurse for the glimpse she'd had of his life, a better friend, a richer woman.

Seven months since they'd met; five weeks since the night he'd made love to her the first time; three since their magnanimous gesture and her freedom to explore life. Her sigh was deep, her mood less buoyant. Were they Sky and Ryan all over again?

While the chamber music played, the guests ate supper and Erin mingled. Marnie Taylor and her husband were present and they gave her a chance to focus on what had brought her to Millbrook in the first place. "I miss the administrative end," Erin confessed. "I never thought I would, but being with you really gave me a chance to sink my teeth into program development. Since the clinic's so much smaller, I really got a fish-eye view of how much is settled in the boardroom. It was stimulating when I was part of it, frustrating now that I'm not." She laughed and shrugged off the wistfulness. "Forgive me. I'm discontent at the moment about a lot of things."

Marnie nodded. "Instinct can play a part, Erin, a sort of second sight. That's what got Sky involved in the first place, her feeling that there wasn't enough available for teenage mothers. She saw the need, pressed her advantage and wound up suggesting you and your program as a place to start."

As they talked, the dance band replaced the quartet and the tables were cleared. Erin and Marnie paused to watch the celebrating couple lead off the dancing and their conversation drew to a close. When Bill Taylor asked his wife to dance, Erin glanced idly around the tent. Kevin was leaning against a pole, talking with Jake and his wife. When his glance met Erin's, he raised his glass in a silent toast. She nodded and smiled, then fought the restlessness he incited.

She wished she hadn't had the clinic discussion. Discontent should be dealt with one aspect of her life at a time. When she looked back at Kevin, he had his back turned and she'd had just enough champagne to regard it as a challenge. When she'd snaked her way to the tent pole, she stood on tiptoe behind him. "Were you going to ask me to dance tonight, or are you afraid of putting your arms around me?" she whispered.

He turned, his grin in place. "I've played with fire enough this summer. You're better off at arm's length. I'm not sure I've got the stamina for another one of Matt's assaults."

"Matt shouldn't have anything to do with this. I thought I made that perfectly clear on the Fourth of July."

He shook his head and the breeze played with his hair. "Erin, where you're concerned, nothing will ever be perfectly clear. You have a way of blurring a man's vision till his common sense oozes down out of his feet and his rational mind disintegrates. I think that's been proven to you on more than one occasion. Sorry, no dancing."

"Conversation?" She leaned back against the pole, flattered.

"I guess I can chance that. I'm glad to hear that you're following my advice. Matt made sure I knew your social life is—how did he put it?—*active*. I expected Greg on your arm tonight. Knowing my brother as well as I do, I wouldn't have been surprised to see you arrive with a phalanx of Harvard types."

She took a long time watching his face. "You blushed when I arrived. Was that relief?"

Kevin knit his brow. "How much champagne have you had?"

"Darling, our relationship is nothing if not painfully honest. I did think about asking Greg. I thought you might want to see for yourself that I'm taking your advice out there in the fast lane. We're too thoughtful, you and I. I like to think that giving me up might not have been all that easy for you, that a couple of things in our week together were memorable. The Fourth of July seemed terribly important to me. I wanted you to see that I was doing fine."

"Oil, medicine, Beverly Hills, I'll say," Kevin said lightly. "He's quite a man."

She grabbed another tulip glass from a passing tray. "He is, but you don't deserve to have Greg or anyone else thrown in your face because of what we can't be together. This is your family, Kevin, and your town. I'm a guest." Erin's throat constricted and she took a quick swallow before things got maudlin. "Maybe you blushed because I'm all dressed up. Do you like this slinky black number? You could have had a date, too. I thought I might have to compete with some gorgeous, mature, Millbrook woman who'd be draped all over you giving me condescending looks."

Spurred on by Kevin's laugh, Erin went back up on her toes. "If you'll loan me your socks, I could positively fall out of this and get you all steamy and passionate."

"Erin, I've already had my jaw realigned for my behavior." He glanced around for his youngest brother, who was talking with Jody.

"I know, I know. The steam and passion are for lovers. We're friends."

With a sigh, Kevin took her glass and set it on the table. "You may get into less trouble on the dance floor than you will if you keep up this line of conversation. God knows, I will." He crooked his elbow and she slipped her arm through.

"Be still, my heart."

Fourteen

Kevin's timing was off. The tempo of the music, which had packed the dance floor, slowed as the band drifted into a fox-trot. He pivoted with his hand in the small of Erin's back as he tried to leave.

"Oh, no, you don't. A friend deserves more than thirty seconds of an old Beach Boys' number." She put her left hand on his shoulder and her right into his left, then looked down at their feet. "Six inches between us. We're safe, nobody'll suspect a thing."

He brought his face next to her cheek. "Keep your voice down."

"If I don't, will you stay this close to me?" Beneath her left hand, his shoulder slumped as he sighed.

"Have you ever in your life behaved yourself and done what you were told?"

Erin stayed the proper distance for three measures before she answered. "Yes. The first night you made love to me, I did exactly what you—'' Three fingers landed softly, but squarely on her lips.

"Not another word."

"I won't talk. I'll fantasize; you can, too."

They danced. It was a slow set and gradually, imperceptibly, their rhythm melded. He led, she followed, no longer stiff and suspicious or coy and challenging. Kevin's touch on the middle of her back was warm and dry. Did he long to urge her closer? Did he recall the feel of her against his chest? Of course he did; reverie was as much the problem as her behavior, she thought.

The musical set ended far too soon and as the band took a break, there was no choice but to leave the floor. "Thank you, that was lovely," she murmured with sudden sincerity.

"You're welcome. Will you walk with me for a while?"

Her heart gave that joyful leap. "I don't suppose you had in mind the spot out there on the edge of the golf course?"

Kevin pointed to the canopy of maples bordering the boxwood. When she'd taken his arm and pulled off her shoes, they started out. "Why don't you hit me with both barrels and get it over with," she said.

When they had some privacy he looked at her but kept strolling. "I want to apologize for what you overheard in the library on the Fourth. I never meant for you to hear. I assume you were in the foyer for most of it."

Her footsteps faltered. "What I heard was your apology to Matt. I'm glad he means so much to you, although I find it absurd to think I could come between any Branigans."

"You have to understand his perspective, Erin. He's the youngest and as protective of you as I was of him. Don't say anything, please! I've practically memorized this little speech, just hear me out." He raked his fingers through his hair with a huff.

"You can call it rites of manhood, or machoism or whatever you like, but there's a certain amount of wild oat sowing that boys do, a certain amount of testing, of proving themselves." He stopped. "I'm no good at this."

"I'm with you so far, verbal expression takes as much practice as sex. Take your time."

"Erin!"

She squeezed his hand. "Just trying to make it easier."

He began to rush. "Matt practically grew up without a woman in the house. Needless to say, I was the one who told him the facts of life, with the rest of them only too happy to explain the finer points. He's known since the age of twelve that he wanted to be a doctor. I'm afraid I drummed into him the importance of holding back on anything permanent until he reached that goal. I've... been a role model in that respect, too. Everything was working fine until Erin O'Connor fell from heaven."

"Kevin, I'm hardly an angel."

"He's not looking for an angel. In some ways he's following old Kevin's example: good times, no strings, with nose to the books in his case. You're the sister he never had, somebody who finally rounds out his view of women. You love him, you care for each other and the best part is there's no chemistry between you, nothing to foul things up. It's perfect just the way it is. Just the way it *was*. Damned insightful, if I do say so myself. Too bad, it hit me this late. To Matthew's way of thinking, I've taken what he cherished and treated her no differently from any of the others. Used is an ugly word, but that's the way he sees it."

Erin was quiet, the leprechaun gone from her behavior. "He's very, very wrong. It's time your brother stopped looking at the world through his tunnel vision. He grew up watching you keep your emotional distance from women, so of course he thinks you're a playboy. I've known that since

I've known him. It didn't help for you to insist our affair
was a mistake and never should have happened.

"It's time he was asked to imagine how much chance you
had to fall in love. When you were in your twenties, when
life is all raw and wonderful, you had custody of your
brothers. When you were the age I am right now, you had a
sixteen-year-old and a thirteen-year-old at home. Not to
mention nineteen-year-old Ryan and his antics," she replied. "What woman in the prime of her dating years would
want to settle down with that? What set of parents would let
their daughter consider it! Emotional commitment was out
of the question; maybe you even chanced it and learned
those facts of life the hard way. What choice have you had
but to separate sex and love?"

"Erin, I don't think—"

"You made me listen, you owe me the same courtesy. I
know what I represent to Matt—a sister—the kind of bond
you share with Annie and Sky and Holly. They're all platonic relationships, free from all the complications you and
I have gotten into."

He turned from her, dead in his tracks, his breath held
tight in his chest. She took his hand in both of hers. "There
I go, delving into your psyche, digging right under those
calluses on your heart." Her throat was dry and tight.
"Kevin, darling, we're beating a dead horse. Stop tripping
over your guilt. You've made a huge difference in my life.
It wasn't a mistake and I don't mind being lumped in with
all those other lucky women."

She grasped at levity as her eyes began to shine with
unshed tears. "According to Matt, you like big bosoms and
lots of experience. I'm flattered to be in that category! Every
woman should have her first affair with someone as wonderful as you." She smiled at his involuntary laugh.

"Kevin, I owe you an apology, too. I've said a lot of presumptuous things. You're a very private man, I should never have called it a facade. I can only imagine what you've coped with, but I have no right to expect you to pour your heart out. It was arrogant of me, maybe a way for me to feel less vulnerable, who knows." This time when the tears welled, she had to press her fingers between her eyes, horrified at her lack of control. "Forgive me, this seems to happen every time we get serious. I'm much better at flirting."

"Just about the best," he said as he pressed a handkerchief into her hand. Kevin stood patiently, silently, as she regained her composure. "Sometimes you seem to know me better than I know myself, Erin. I find that rather amazing after all these years." He looked back toward the music and guests. "I think we've said all there is to say this time. Before we turn each other inside out, would you like to dance?"

She shook her head and worked her feet back into her sandals as they approached the patio. "No, I don't think so."

"I'm leaving Tuesday, Erin. I have an open-ended invitation to do some fishing in the Adirondacks. The whole month of August is open if I want it. Jody's coming home since Drew and Sean are leaving, too. They're going to Maine."

"Yes, Sky mentioned the vacations."

"Even I need to get away from the bogs and the house once in a while," Kevin said.

"Will you be alone, you and the stream and some rustic cabin?" She put up her hand. "Don't answer that, my curiosity's done enough damage already." He didn't. He didn't even smile. He just sighed wistfully, leaving Erin to imagine what Kevin had prescribed for himself in the way of remedy.

She left him there and headed for Sky, who was watching Ryan in discussion with a Millbrook detective. "Shop talk," she said to Erin, "they used to work the same shift at the station."

"It's a lovely party," Erin offered. "Do you ever regret that it took so long to get together?"

Sky shook her head. "We were too different, too young, and worlds apart back then. When the infatuation wore off—and it always does, Erin—we would have resented the boundaries we'd made for each other. It doesn't matter what the gulf is. Money, social position, education, age, anything that stands in the way has to be resolved in your own mind. There's no man or woman perfect enough to make it happen for you. The danger is that quick affairs get you so infatuated you think nothing matters but being together." She looked lovingly at her fiancé as he moved away with the fellow officer.

"Ryan will always be a cop and a cranberry grower and I'll always be a debutante. At eighteen I would have convinced myself that loving him was the ultimate sacrifice." She put her fist to her breast. "Goodbye Beacon Hill, goodbye Palm Beach, for Ryan, anything. It would have lasted six months. Marriage is built on compromise not sacrifice."

Sky looped her arm through Erin's and lowered her voice. "Are we really talking about Ryan and me? We couldn't possibly be discussing you and the man I found spitting blood into my kitchen sink on the Fourth of July? The one who's been biting everybody's head off since you left Millbrook?"

"He and Matt had an argument," Erin tried.

"He and Matt, he and Ryan, he and Drew; he growls at his dogs. The man has a heart the size of Wyoming, but it's always had barbed wire around it. Into his life comes a fire-cracker with a pair of metal cutters. She's too young, too educated, too savvy, too starry-eyed and way, way too in-nocent. Erin, Kevin's been run over by pixie dust and he's frantically trying to brush it off."

"You knew! Does everybody else?" Erin whispered.

Ryan broke from his conversation and Sky patted Erin's arm. "I'm a woman; you and I have been friends since New Year's Eve. I read it in you long before I saw it in Kevin. The rest of the bunch just think he's overstressed from the busi-ness." She smiled as Ryan took her in his arms and the con-versation died.

When the evening ended, Erin was tempted to persuade Matt to return to Marlborough Street instead of the bogs, but she was in no mood to risk more of her roommate's wrath and suspicion. Instead, when they wound their way over the Duxbury Road to the Branigan lane, she made small talk about the clinic.

The house, which she'd known only as peacefully mas-culine, had the air of a fraternity. Matt watched as the dogs greeted her and she helped herself to a glass of cranberry juice from the refrigerator. "You certainly feel at home," he quipped.

She was seated at the kitchen table, her bare legs up on the chair next to her, when Jody arrived with Kevin. They pulled back the screen and she looked out on the porch at the empty spot where her sneakers had sat in June. By the time Ryan came in, she was chewing the ice in her empty glass.

There was much loosening of ties and popping of cuff links as they draped their dinner jackets over the chairs. Kevin talked about the barn and Ryan talked about his fu-ture in-laws. Between business and reminiscence, Erin had nothing to offer. The way Kevin looked with his dress shirt rolled up over his forearms and open at the throat altered everything going on beneath her slip of a cocktail dress. She picked up her sandals and her overnight bag. "Kevin, if you'll just tell me which bed I'm in, I'll go on up."

The innocent remark turned four handsome faces in her direction. Three looked back at Kevin. Conversation stopped; color mottled his cheeks. "Jody's old room. He can double up in the bunks with Matt," he answered tersely.

"Good night," they called in unison, waiting, she was sure, for her to climb the stairs before the teasing began. Jody and Ryan would tease. Matt would sit and scowl. When her light was out, she lay in Jody's bed and listened to the family sounds in the house that had held them so long, Kevin's empty nest. When they climbed the stairs the second floor came to life. The sounds of furniture scraping came from the next room. Matt and Jody talked. Somebody was whistling...muffled laughter...the shower. She sighed into her pillow. It was time to go home.

Sunday morning was interminable. She ate breakfast with the four of them. Every glance seemed furtive, every remark a double entendre. A *je ne sais quoi* in the air hung like an umbrella. She went to church alone and stared from the front steps across the common to Schuyler House. The driveway held cars with out-of-state license plates; the carriage barn was freshly painted. Ryan had returned to Kevin's for the duration. He was compromising.

Matt and Erin said their goodbyes to Kevin and the others at the bogs. He made no move to see her alone but carried her luggage to the car. "Have a good fishing trip," Erin said.

"I intend to. I'll see you after the harvest at the wedding, three or four months from now." Kevin smiled at her and touched her hair and then turned and shook Matt's hand. "Use the place if you want. I'll be back by Labor Day."

They were all playing by Kevin's rules.

Fifteen

Erin's life was filled to the brim in August. She picnicked on Cape Ann, sailed twice in Marblehead and made excursions to the tennis championships at Longwood Cricket Club in Chestnut Hill. With every invitation and new experience, Kevin's wisdom grew more evident. She wondered often if he stood alone in some icy stream and felt the same about her insight or whether he'd felt the need to take a companion to block out her memory. She looked forward to the day when her love for someone else would make friendship with him possible.

Matt took to studying with a woman in his class and his August nights in his own bed were rare. It was a month nearly devoid of the mention of the name Branigan. The week before Labor Day, she returned from work to the ringing of the phone and even that no longer set her heart racing. Marnie Taylor, on the pretext of business in the city, asked her to dinner.

They'd agreed to a sidewalk café on Newbury Street for the following night and Erin arrived to find Marnie and Winifred Montgomery sipping sweet vermouth at a corner table. They shook hands warmly. "This is a wonderful surprise. No crisis, I hope," Erin said as she took her seat.

Dr. Montgomery shook her head. "The program's going beautifully and our childbirth preparation classes are being recommended by the area of OB/GYNs for all their maternity patients more than a thirty-minute drive east of the hospital. We're already seeing patients who wouldn't have bothered before."

"Erin, we're here for a reason," Marnie added. "The chief of Obstetrics at Plymouth General has accepted a position at Johns Hopkins. Winnie's been approved as his replacement starting December first."

Erin raised her glass. "Congratulations!"

Dr. Montgomery smiled. "I've accepted with mixed feelings. I've been devoted to the auxiliary program in Millbrook as if it were another baby to deliver. In all fairness to the clinic and my family, however, I'm going to have to resign everything but my position on the board."

Erin's heart began to thump. "You've been invaluable."

"No one's irreplaceable. We want you to consider taking on the position of director. You'd work as an assistant to the clinic director with the program directors under you. It's small enough with ample opportunity for you to teach if you want to maintain your patient contact. We need someone with administrative education. I'm a practicing physician. If possible, we'd like you to come on while I'm still there, so we can overlap for two months. Erin, we need exactly what you've already given us in Women's Services. It carries a straight salary, with additional fees for teaching. Your salary would increase by about a third to start."

"This is quite a surprise," Erin replied. "Millbrook . . . when, exactly?"

"Mid-September would give you three weeks to conclude current obligations and eight weeks with Winnie. If you accept, we need a two-year commitment for the sake of continuity since the programs will be phasing in over the next year."

"I had no idea. How am I expected to eat dinner!"

"Think it over. We'd like a decision within twenty-four hours. Obviously you're our first choice but because of the timing, anyone we ask should have the same three-week cushion to pull out of current obligations."

"Of course," Erin replied, dipping limply into her salad.

She couldn't have told anyone what she'd eaten, she didn't recall dessert. They talked nonstop through the meal, analyzing the opportunity from every professional angle. It didn't mean leaving Marlborough Street. The commute was little more than an hour. Marnie joked about the Boston nightlife in comparison to the bucolic atmosphere in Millbrook. "Hardly a place for a twenty-four-year-old to be single, I suppose."

How ironic, she thought for the hundredth time when she'd finally gotten to bed. It was her social life that caused the hesitation.

Erin put in a full shift at the hospital the following day, stayed in the cafeteria for dinner and taught her childbirth class at seven-thirty. At ten she had Matt paged on the Maternity wing and watched him stumble bleary-eyed from the physicians' sleeping room. "Hi stranger," she chirped as he studied her. "I thought all these nights you and your new love were reading bedtime stories in her apartment."

"Wishful thinking. What's up?"

"I need a thoroughly unbiased opinion about my medical future."

Matt snapped to attention and glanced at his watch. "I can give you half an hour. The sleeping room's empty."

They went back into the bunk room reserved for cat-naps, Matt on the lower bunk, Erin in a hard-backed chair. She gave him her prepared speech. "I've had two members of a board approach me about taking on the administra-tion of a program for women and children. It's a smaller version of what we do here, small enough for me to teach some, as well as oversee the implementation of the pro-grams, something I'll never get to do if I stay here."

"Big fish in a little pond?"

"Yes. More money, too."

"How secure is the little pond?" he asked, yawning.

"Firm. Impeccable reputation, established program, well funded, and affiliated with the local hospital. It's within commuting distance, too, so I wouldn't have to relocate."

"And you're just telling me now?"

Erin patted his arm. "We're ships in the night, these days. I just got the offer yesterday."

"Go for it. Sounds like a plum. Where is it?"

She cleared her throat. "It's the Millbrook clinic."

"You can't be serious! I thought you meant a satellite clinic in the North End or Chinatown. Erin, you're out of your mind. I thought you stopped making a fool of your-self last June. There can only be one reason why you'd even consider Millbrook."

Erin was stung by his remarks. "I know how this must look, but it has nothing to do with Kevin, absolutely noth-ing. In fact, if I accept the offer, I want your word that you won't mention it to your family."

"You've never been interested in administration. If this is some last-ditch effort—"

She pointed her finger at him. "Stop thinking like a Branigan! I may have been briefly involved with your brother, but I'm not foolish enough to jeopardize my career for him or any other man. This is a chance to put my graduate work into practice. My first shot at that was in Millbrook. Matt, look at you. How much thought did you ever give to obstetrics until you took the rotation? You were going to be an internist. Shall I accuse you of changing your mind because I let you practice a breast exam on me and now you want to be in my department? What you're suggesting about Kevin is just as ridiculous. This is medicine, the reason I went to Millbrook in the first place."

He arched his eyebrows and relaxed. "If Kevin has no bearing on this, why am I sworn to secrecy?"

"Because he'll think the way you do."

"The commute'll kill you."

"I can sublet and get something closer."

"You can't keep this quiet. Sky volunteers there. It's next to the bogs!"

"The point is, Matt, this is an independent decision; Erin O'Connor doing what's best for Erin O'Connor. There was life before Branigans and there'll be life after. If and when Kevin finds out, it'll be his problem."

Erin made one more call and that was to London. Nancy concurred. Nancy had no idea about life as Erin had been living it, which made her approval all the more valuable. She, too, saw it as a good business decision.

Erin talked with the head of the Nursing department. It was a gut reaction; it felt right. She called Marnie at her home after dinner and accepted.

There wasn't any fanfare until the end. She worked the final weeks of August and the first of September happily, as dedicated to her patients as ever. Her closest friends took her to lunch but since she wasn't moving, there was no regret, just expectation. Matt made a point of being home the morning of the fifteenth and they ate breakfast together, toasting the clinic with orange juice. "I hope it turns out perfectly," he said.

She grinned. "A woman's gotta do what a woman's gotta do."

She put up with the emotional tug when her commute put her in familiar territory. She drove past the bogs next to the golf course aware that the berries had set and were ripening. Harvesting would begin in a month. At the clinic she was officially welcomed and given an office. The workload was considerable. "The luxury of having an assistant is that she gets the thankless job of troubleshooting," Winnie told her, honest enough to lay out the difficult tasks first.

Erin took on the scheduling for the rest of the calendar year, which entailed coordinating rooms, instructors, patients and class size. What she hoped would become second nature demanded hours of concentration as she sorted through the paperwork.

Erin had had the foresight to call Sky and ask for her silence about the appointment. Her friend had reacted the way Matt had, but promised to keep her end of the request. She'd also assured Erin that from now until the last berry was delivered to the processing plant in Middleboro, her whereabouts would escape anybody's thoughts. All of the Millbrook Branigans had business on their minds. The conversation took place shortly after Labor Day and Sky's return from Nantucket. When they met face-to-face at the clinic, Sky hugged her and grinned. "I take it August was full of soul searching?"

"Only from a professional standpoint," Erin replied.

"Professional. I see. I assume that's why Kevin spent three weeks in the wilds of New York State talking to the trout. It improved his business sense."

"If you don't mind, I'd like to change the subject and get back to work," Erin added.

Sky had the audacity to wink as she left the office and the compassion to drop the subject in the days that followed. Erin had enough to keep her occupied.

Her third week in Millbrook, the weather snapped. It was a New England trait at the end of September which brought continually frosty nights even with balmy afternoons. Summer was gone and the slow descent of the thermometer meant that cranberries were ripening in every corner of the county.

On Tuesday morning Erin passed the Corvette and the Bronco as they pulled off Duxbury Road onto the edge of the bogs beyond the clinic and the country club. The sand-pile was smaller, the access widened and graded as Kevin had said it would be. A backhoe sat on the dike. The screen of green foliage was beginning to yellow and crimson peeked from the encroaching woodlands. Erin wondered if any of the family had the time to enjoy the beautiful changes. She wondered who would take the shifts when the frost threatened and they monitored the sprinkler systems all night.

In the next two weeks the foliage became dramatic in its brilliance and Erin became acclimated to her job. She loved the novelty of pulling together a polished wardrobe since she was without uniforms for the first time. She was in a teal-blue sweaterdress the October morning she knocked on Winnie's door and was told to enter.

Kevin Branigan, in full pinstripe business suit and club tie, was sitting in the chair facing the doctor. He stopped in midsentence.

"Excuse me, I had no idea you had someone with you," Erin blurted.

Surprise and confusion clouded Kevin's features, but Winnie was the one who spoke. "This concerns you, come right in! You know Kevin Branigan, of course. We've been discussing a generous donation in the name of the corporation. Branigan Cranberries has offered to underwrite a portion of the parenting program."

Kevin got to his feet and smoothed down his tie before he shook her hand. "This is a surprise. Are you doing more consulting?"

Erin swallowed.

"Better than that. Erin's come on as director of Women's Services. She's assisting me and will take over in December. She's been here about a month."

"A month," he repeated.

Two months of normal pulse rates vanished. Her heart raced until she could hear it, while she watched him arch his brows in that bemused way of his. "These are for you," she said suddenly, handing the files to Winnie. "Sorry I interrupted. Nice to see you again, Kevin."

Ten minutes later, in the privacy of her own office, Erin sat at her desk with her fingers on her wrist. She took her own pulse while she closed her eyes and did some deep breathing exercises. When her door was opened without a knock, she took her feet off her desk and opened her eyes.

Kevin closed the door behind him. "We can't have anyone out there suspecting you of anxiety."

"It's the job, lots of pressure," she said quickly.

He sat on the edge of her desk, his hands resting on his pinstriped thigh. "Administering Women's Services for about a month. Just how many of my family members were sworn to secrecy?"

"There's no secret to this, Kevin." He seemed to be enjoying the cut of her sweaterdress as she spoke.

"Maybe not. About a week ago I could have sworn I passed you in your car while I was turning onto the bogs. I even mentioned it to Sky and Ryan at dinner. She accused me of not being able to get you off my mind."

"How absurd."

"That's what I told her. 'We're not even friends,' I said. Ryan accused me of worse, but then Ryan and I rarely see eye-to-eye on anything first time around. How about Matthew? Are you down here with his blessing? There can't be many neurosurgeons in Millbrook."

Erin shifted in her chair and wished he weren't quite so close. "Matt agreed this was an excellent professional opportunity. I'm still living on Marlborough Street. My social life's just fine."

"So he still tells me at every opportunity. Not that I ask," he added.

"How was your vacation in the Adirondacks?" She'd been looking past him, but when Erin glanced up, their eyes reflected something deep, identical... and unrecognized.

"It was refreshing, having the last word."

She nodded. "Then you weren't alone?"

"The couple who own the cabin were there the first and last weekends. The rest of the time I communed with the trout stream." A smiled played over his lips. "There's a retreat on the way out there, and the damnedest thing happened. I saw a group of nuns strolling under the trees in their billowy habits. I remembered your commenting about them on Beacon Hill. It got me to thinking about that afternoon, when I walked you from Sky's house back to Marlborough Street." He was still looking into her wide brown eyes and her pulse was still perking in her wrists. "You really didn't want me to know about this job?"

She came to her senses. "Can't you see why? Good Lord, Kevin, if I'd had any idea what lay in store when I let Nancy talk me into living with her and that red-blooded Irishman with all the brothers..." She let the sentence drift.

Kevin stood up. "Took us both by surprise. It's a dead horse, I know that, but what a ride!"

She straightened up and smoothed the bodice of her sweaterdress. "Kevin Branigan, are you flirting with me?"

He shook his head. "Feels like it. The damnedest things happen when I get near you. I'd love to continue this, but I'm due back. This time of year gets crazy. Too much work to be done." He walked from her and opened the door. "I'm sorry you still felt the need to keep this from me."

Erin stayed at her desk and shuffled papers. "Kevin, it was my work that brought me to Boston and Matt, and my work that brought me down here. Now would you please go back to yours so I can get back to mine?"

He nodded in complete agreement. "Sometimes your advice is right on the mark. The last thing I need this time of year is some perky little creature ruining what sleep I can get."

They stared, the meaningful glance between them diamond bright despite the words from either of them.

Sixteen

The episode ruined Erin for the rest of the day. She lost her train of thought in midsentence, took twice the normal amount of time to finish a task and vainly tried to ignore the fact that her emotions had, once again, taken on a life of their own.

The warm sparkle of Millbrook in autumn didn't help. The sky was cloudless, a robin's-egg blue over bogs whose flooded surface splintered the reflected light into gemlike brilliance. Sugar maples, heavy with yellow leaves, hung over the country roads and her car kicked up trails of crimson and gold from what had fallen. It was a good time to fall in love, better than the green promise of spring or the lethargic days of summer. This was the season for snuggling.

"I'm losing my mind," she muttered while stalled in traffic. "I must be a masochist." Nothing had changed between them, not his denial of her, not her desire for him.

How dare Kevin! How could he just invade her office, casually drape himself on the edge of her desk and insinuate?

How could he? Maybe it was some compulsion to see if the spark still ignited, to see how much self-control he still possessed, to see how much good his weeks in the wilderness had done. A slow, delicious grin started across her face as she drove north toward Boston. Then again, maybe Kevin Branigan, for all his maturity and wisdom, was still fighting his own compulsions.

When she finally dragged herself from the car and unlocked 319 Marlborough Street she was no better off than when she'd left the clinic, with the exception of one shred of insight. Five minutes in the presence of Kevin Branigan felt better than days with anyone else.

"So the cat's out of the bag," Sky said the next day over yogurt in the small lunchroom. "Kevin's words were a little more graphic. He's not thrilled when he feels his family's conspiring against him, family meaning me."

"Sky, I don't want you involved in this," Erin replied.

"It's a pleasure. I thought you might want to know that he and I were sitting at my table in the kitchen. He brought it up over coffee." She cleared and lowered her voice. "'Sky, I'm sorry you felt you couldn't tell me Erin was back at the clinic.' 'She asked me not to. Does that bother you?' I said. He swore it didn't, but he also poured cream into the sugar instead of his mug." Sky was grinning. "He's been nobly sacrificing for so long, he can't figure out why this magnanimous gesture hurts so much."

"Did he tell you that?"

Sky scoffed. "Kevin? He'd sell a bog first. I know those furtive glances, those deep sighs. He and Ryan can carry on whole conversations just by raising their eyebrows. I want to give you one bit of unsolicited advice. When you called and told me you'd taken this job, you said it felt right; it was a gut reaction. If this thing with Kevin feels the same, don't let him slip through your fingers. He can't wait fourteen years for you to come around again."

Erin ate dinner with Matt that evening in the coziness of their apartment. "Matt, if you could wish anything for me in the world, *one thing*, what would it be?"

"Why?"

"One thing," she repeated.

"Happiness, of course."

"And what would you wish for Kevin?"

"I knew it. Honestly, Erin, this Millbrook thing will ruin you."

"No, this Millbrook thing will be the source of that happiness. I've been truthful with you about all of this, but I've been lying to myself, and Kevin's the biggest liar of all. He loves me Matt, the real kind, he just doesn't know it. Or worse, he can't admit it because it seems so inappropriate. He's gotten some dumb idea that it will keep me from what life has to offer, from experiencing The World. You seem to have the same idea. Your big, rock of a brother, the foundation of the family, is pushing me as if I were the law student or the medical student or the recalcitrant cop. He may very well know what's good for all of you, but I, Erin Flynn O'Connor am what's good for *him* and he's what's good for me."

Matt groaned. "You're hallucinating."

"Of course I am, I'm in love. I love that man with everything I've got and I know he loves me the same way. Trust me on this...I'm not sneaking around, or lying to you or denying anything. You mean the world to me and if you want my happiness, you'll accept my feelings as true and valuable and let me do what has to be done."

"I'm afraid to ask."

"I want your word that you'll keep this to yourself until I've had a chance to bring it out in the open."

"How long will that be, pray tell?"

"Not long, darling roommate, not long."

For forty-eight hours after their encounter, Erin didn't hear from Kevin. She hadn't expected to. Wednesday morning on the way to work, she found a florist in Plymouth and bought a single red rose. She put it in the refrigerator at the clinic and took Sky aside. "I'd like to have it resting on the front seat of his Corvette about five tonight, so I'll be gone when he finds it. Instinct will tell him it's from me, common sense will say it can't be."

Sky was delighted. "Let Holly in on this. She's always been able to tease him. She'd love to be part of this, Annie, too."

"Let's take care of the rose, first. I've got real work to do." Erin laughed.

Sky agreed. "For now, a single rose. He'll quit about sundown; you'll be on the expressway by then."

She was on the expressway, stuck in traffic, grinning like a happy cat, when the sun fell behind the western cityscape. Matt was gone when she got home, but there was a note.

Sky called. Mission accomplished. She refused to give me details. I'm not sure I want any.

XXX, Matt

Erin drew on discipline she didn't know she had and threw herself into her breast-feeding classes. She spent hours with Winnie, praying she didn't appear distracted, if anything, giving more to her job to compensate for the thrill of turning Kevin around.

Thursday passed without a word and Sky reported that Kevin had neither mentioned the rose nor even looked at her askance. "I think you should know he has a date tonight. Nothing serious at all, but he is going out with a mutual friend's sister. Friday night supper."

"Does Holly have access to the house?" Erin asked without a twinge of guilt. She held up a single after-dinner mint, wrapped in foil with elegant gold script. Sky's eyes shone. "Ms. Schuyler, you're enjoying this more than I am," Erin said. She handed over the mint. "Have Holly roll down his bed covers, neatly...and put the bedside lamp on. This on the pillow. It doesn't have any significance to us, simply a romantic gesture."

"Keep in mind, the man's running on very little sleep. He's up at the bogs all night sometimes, working sunup to sundown the rest of the time," Sky said.

"I'll give it a week."

Kevin gave it less than twenty-four hours. Saturday morning at nine, Matt picked up the phone. "It's Kevin," he called to Erin, who had ducked into the bathroom. "He wants to speak with you."

"Take a message, tell him I'm about to get in the shower." She yanked on the faucets for effect.

"He says to wrap up in something and get out here."

She pulled on a robe and ignored Matt's glower. "Kevin, how are you?"

After a sigh he said, "Fine. Erin, have you been to the house?"

She was instantly concerned. "Your house, of course not. Is something wrong? Kevin, is something missing, have you had a robbery?"

"Erin..."

She smiled at the hesitation in his voice. How on earth would he bring this up? "Kevin, you know I would never let myself into your house without telling you. Why would you ask *me*?''

"It seemed like your sense of humor." He sounded embarrassed.

"A joke's better than a robbery, I guess. Here, would you tell Matt about it? I've got a date for squash at the Radcliffe courts and I'm just about to jump in the shower. Let's have lunch one day after the harvest. It was fun seeing you that day at the clinic. Here's Matt." Without waiting for his reply, she handed the phone to her roommate and went back to her shower.

When she finally emerged from the bathroom, Matt was at his books. "Care to tell me what that was all about?" he asked.

"He didn't say?"

"Only that if I heard the details, he'd be risking a broken jaw. Erin, what have you been up to?"

"Helping a perfectly wonderful man come to his senses."

Erin filled her weekend with friends, though the hours dragged and her mood was too volatile for her to concentrate on much of anything. Monday morning Sky was waiting in her office. "I'm ready for my next assignment."

"How'd you like to invite me as a houseguest at the end of the week, if I live that long."

"We'd love to have you at Schuyler House. If you ever get tired of the commute, neighbors of ours are looking for someone to rent their converted carriage house. It's a charming one bedroom, three doors from mine. It's reasonable, too. Should this escalate, you might want to have a place of your own right here."

Erin laughed. "I like the way you think." After the rose and the chocolate, Erin knew Kevin would be on edge, suspecting a third memento. She didn't do a thing. Wednes-

day, five days after the tidbit on his pillow, Kevin called Erin
and asked her to lunch.

"Can you possibly take the time? What would Ryan
say?"

"A man's got to eat," he replied. At twelve-thirty, un-
announced, he stuck his head in her door. Still dressed for
work, he had on a thick, cabled sweater, its turtleneck
skimming his jaw. A green, down vest wrapped his chest and
his pants were worn cords the color of wheat. He wore his
ancient boat shoes, and there was a twig in his hair.

Erin tugged it out playfully as she grabbed her purse and
snapped off the light. "This reminds me of the time you
found pine needles in my hair," she whispered as they went
through the reception room.

He threw her the Corvette keys and got into the passenger side. "May I ask why you said that?"

Erin slipped the key into the ignition. "No reason. It's
one of my favorite memories. I get to drive?"

"Sure, it's another of your favorite memories, I'll bet."

Over the purr of the engine, they smiled at each other and
then she drove to the grill he suggested nearby. He's hint-
ing. He's desperate for me to give myself away, she told
herself, steeling her heart against the joy of the moment.

They ate hamburgers and French fries in a booth while
she watched the clientele, mostly tradesmen and men on the
road, come and go. "I guess we're not apt to run into any of
your family in here."

He flushed so suddenly, she grew hot herself. "I thought
you might want to talk," he muttered, searching her face for
answers to questions he couldn't ask.

She munched a French fry. "That never did us any good
at all, Kevin, I seemed to always wind up in tears. You
brought my eager little body to life with yours night after
night and then made me see how much more of life lay

ahead. My goodness, since then I've really started taking
advantage of Boston. The city just pulsates." She took another bite.

"It's funny, I'll be playing tennis or taking a shower and
I can almost feel your touch. No, we had an affair to remember, as they say, but I don't want to dwell on it. That's
why I went to such lengths to keep my job down here separate from you." Maintaining a bland expression took the
skill of a thespian. Kevin's color was deep, his eyes bright
with what she knew were mental images vividly recalled. "I
hope it won't bother you if I join you on Saturday. I know
you didn't invite me specifically, but Matt's coming down
for the harvesting and he thought I might like to help out,
get a first-hand look. If you have a date, I wouldn't mind.
You owe me one, after I threw Greg under your nose. You
are dating?"

"Occasionally."

"Sky tells me there'll be chowder and carrying-on, a
Branigan tradition after you finish the bogs at the house."

"Yes." Full sentences seemed a problem. He cleared his
throat. "Have you seen Holly lately?"

"No, not since the engagement party. Could she have
gotten into the house and played whatever that joke was?
Why don't you tell me about it."

He shook his head. "No point."

Erin looked at her watch. "I should get back."

She drove to the clinic, lingering in the driver's seat just
long enough to thank him for lunch. "Good to see you
again. You look so handsome all bundled up for the
weather. It seems like yesterday that you were making love
to me in the woods, right where you'll be harvesting this
weekend. Can you believe it was hot enough that night for
us to have been naked right out there. Of course I was warm
since you were on top. You can't say I wasn't an eager stu-

dent, Kevin Branigan. Well, got to run. Thanks so much fo
lunch. I haven't let you get a word in, I'm sorry, it's one o
my worst habits. Next time, you can talk!''

She was out of the car and into the clinic before he left the
parking spot. Kevin would now drive back to his brothers ir
a state of semishock, knowing in his heart of hearts that she
was up to something, that she was playing with fire and that
she was loving it. Unless he was still so caught up in his
conception of her as innocent and wide-eyed, that lunch
would forever seem a jumble of conversation that he'd mis-
interpreted.

Erin entered the administrative offices, walked directly
into the ladies' room and splashed cold water on her face in
hopes the shock would lessen her internal upheaval. She'd
probably give herself a stroke and after her recent display,
she'd deserve it.

Seventeen

Friday reinforced Erin's feeling that life, occasionally, was perfect. Kevin had his suspicions. Erin had packed for a quick stay at Schuyler House and frost was forecasted. It was perfect. Sky reported that Ryan and Kevin were the ones to monitor the bogs during the night.

Her day at the clinic finished with a staff meeting and she was jubilant as she drove to Sky's. Ryan made them all drinks, which they sipped in front of the fire in the Schuyler House library as dinner simmered. The night was clear and calm and the 4:00 p.m. report from the Frost Warning Service predicted a dip to the twenties. "Holly's bogs by the golf course are finished. Tonight we'll spray everything else. The decision has to be made six hours ahead," Ryan explained to Erin. "Drew'll take a drive before he goes to bed and I'll pick up Kevin and monitor after that."

"Could I come along and take a look?" Erin asked innocently.

"Makes for a long night."

Sky touched Ryan's arm. "She's invited to help tomor row, this is another aspect it's nice to see once anyway. Don' mention it to Kevin if he calls, Ry. He's so grouchy he's ap to say no and I don't want you two in another argument."

Ryan shrugged. "Does he know you're in town?"

"He knows I'll be there tomorrow."

"It might be nice to have you along, force him to be pleasant. The last woman forced along was Holly two years ago, when Drew made her get a close look at the operation. According to Kevin he spent the whole trip kissing her. If the mood strikes, throw your arms around Kevin yourself. The man needs something to kick him out of his moodiness."

"I might just do that," Erin replied.

That night, at one o'clock, there was a soft tap on Erin's bedroom door. "This is your last chance to back out," Sky whispered.

"Not on your life." Fully alert, Erin dressed as the men would, in heavy sweaters and flannel over jeans and thick socks. She did, however, add the cologne that had lingered more than once on Kevin's pillow. When she'd brushed out her hair, she grabbed her gloves and ski parka and went downstairs to join Ryan.

As he drove the Bronco through town and out to Kev-in's, he turned to look at Erin. "I don't suppose you want to tell me what you and the debutante are up to?"

"Up to?"

Ryan laughed. "I'm a former cop. I'm also male and we're not quite as unsuspecting as you might think."

"With one notable exception," Erin said with a grin.

Ryan drove down the hill and idled the engine in front of the house. The kitchen light was on, Kevin moved in front of the window. "Erin, sweetheart, there's only one thing more important to my oldest brother than his business and hat's the family. You're getting a dose of what the rest of us have had all our lives, and that I-know-what's-best-for-you syndrome is a hard habit to break. The man's in love and he can't stand it.'' They both watched as Kevin came out, pulling the door closed behind him. ''If you tell him I told you, I'll leave you out there on the bogs, but, as Drew says, it's about time somebody knocked his socks off.''

She scooted over next to Ryan as the passenger door opened.

''What the hell?''

''Hi, there,'' Erin replied, waving her gloved fingers. ''I was in the neighborhood and I thought I'd come along tonight and see what all this cranberry business is about.''

When he stood his ground, Ryan finally barked, ''Get in!'' He did.

Once up the hill, Erin looked at Drew's house. ''Holly told me all about her first excursion with Drew. Sky was kind enough to invite me to stay at her house.''

''Holly and Sky. Holly, Sky and Erin. The fog's clearing,'' Kevin muttered.

''It's a clear night. Ryan tells me a clear, calm night can give you the most trouble.''

Kevin looked across her. ''Ryan said that?''

''Cranberries, Kev, I was talking about cranberries,'' Ryan shot back.

They drove out of town to the first set of bogs, flat, rectangular patches of gray under a rising moon. Erin sat while the men on either side of her talked business and watched the nearest sprinklers with hand-held flashlights or the wash of the Bronco's headlights. Simultaneously, they slid from the seats and waited for her. Erin chose Kevin's side.

She huddled into her jacket as they walked the dike and checked the pump house, explaining as they went the delicacy of the system. Kevin ran the beam of his flashlight into the blackness for her and talked about the gravity-fed operation of the flumes and the thirteen-hundred-dollar-per-acre system.

There was animation in his conversation, excitement in his expressions as he tugged Erin with him and knelt at the edge of the ditch. He rifled the plants for a handful of berries. "These are the best keeping berry by far. The fruit'll hold through quite a few sprayings. That's what makes them so delicate, Erin. The more we spray for frost protection, the poorer the storage quality. It's always a gamble." He looked out beyond her into the darkness, his breath coming in gray puffs against the whoosh of the water pumps. "Hardly seems like two years since I had Holly out here, trying to drill this into her. And look at her now!"

Erin touched his arm as they stood back up. "Branigans have a way of doing that to women."

Kevin turned to her expectantly, amused, maybe worried. She was exhausted from trying to decipher his expressions. They stared at each other for a full five seconds and then she put her arms around his neck. Without a word he kissed her, softly, his lips warm and pliant. "I've missed you," she whispered. "I've tried so hard not to. I've done everything you wanted me to. I marched right out of your life but I keep looking back. I've honestly been having fun, with wonderful people, but always, I want so much for you to be with us, for you to hear the joke, to see the movie, share the laughs."

He pulled her roughly against his chest, into the wool of his jacket, as if it hurt to listen. She could feel the heaviness of his sigh. He put his gloved hands on her temples as she raised her face to him. "Erin, you've turned my life upside down. Here I am at thirty-seven trying to convince a woman to say *no* to me! I should have more self-control at my age but you've got my hormones in overdrive. This is crazy."

"It's love, Kevin. You and I are in love."

"Is it? It feels like a stake's been driven through my chest. Lordy, Erin, one minute I can't believe what's coming out of that innocent mouth of yours and the next thing I know you're making me hyperventilate. When you and a man break off a relationship, you don't go to lunch with him weeks and weeks later and reminisce about being naked in the woods. It does terrible things to a man's system."

"*If* that man still has inclinations for a roll in the pine needles with her."

"Oh, God."

"That man from the summer is listening, Kevin. He wants *you* to listen to your heart instead of your common sense. This truce we've called, this desperate denial, can't be the right thing. It hurts too much to be right."

A beam of light bounced off his shoulder as Ryan approached, whistling off-key and grinning the Branigan grin. "Sorry folks, but the feeling's gone from my toes no matter what's going on in yours. Had I known what you had in mind, I would have brought Sky along or curled up in the Bronco with the dogs."

They left Duxbury Road and headed for the second set of bogs on the other side of the village. "Take her home on the way," Kevin said to his brother, "I think she's accomplished what she set out to do." He said it with a sardonic smile.

At Schuyler House, Ryan idled the Bronco, said he'd be home within the hour and waited while Kevin walked her to the door. "We have to talk, Erin. I can't get away and come to Boston, lunch was nearly impossible. I'll see you tomorrow for the harvesting, maybe after supper we can grab some time alone."

"I'd like that."

He closed his eyes as if her expression, even in the shadowed light of Sky's lantern, was too much to bear responsibility for. "I'll see you tomorrow," he whispered.

When they'd gone and Erin stood alone in Sky's kitchen, she tapped her foot. She was running on pure adrenaline and instinct, neither of which had ever failed her. She woke Sky long enough to borrow a house key to Kevin's, tell her what she had in mind and thank her. Her palms were sweating by the time she eased her car out onto Millbrook's sleeping streets.

The harvest moon was high and bright enough for her to turn off her headlights as she drove the car at a crawl past Drew and Holly's and down the hill. When she'd parked it in the empty bay in the barn used for the equipment now in use, she let herself into Kevin's house, ruffled the dogs and tiptoed upstairs.

Her heart beat so violently it hurt and she pressed both hands against her ribs. The house was cold, the heat lowered for the night and she shivered as she entered Kevin's room. The bed was as he'd left it, the covers thrown open, illuminated by the brittle moonlight.

Erin left her clothes on his chair and pulled on the nylon gown stuffed into her pocketbook. She stood, shaking from head to toe at the foot of his bed. "No, it's all wrong," she whispered against the anxiety.

Making her way by moonlight, she went into Ryan's room and found the pajamas she'd borrowed once before. An hour later, when the whine of the Bronco signaled the men's return, she lay under Kevin's quilt, in Ryan's pajama top, as anxious and determined as she'd ever been in her life.

She squeezed her eyes shut as the kitchen door opened and held her breath at the sound of Kevin's footsteps on the stairs. The sound of the Bronco disappeared up the hill; she pulled the bed covers to her chin.

Light, blinding it seemed, flooded the room. She cringed. "What in the name of St. Patrick's mother..." He was looking at the nightgown draped at the foot of the bed and the cascade of her rich, red hair on the pillow as she forced her eyes open.

"It's not what you think," she croaked.

"Erin O'Connor, I'm beyond thinking."

She sat up. "See, I'm decent. These are Ryan's. I didn't think it was proper to rummage through your drawers."

"Proper!"

"Kevin, please," she began, but her voice broke and she pressed her fingers against her lips praying for witticisms that would salvage the moment. Instead a flush mottled her cheeks and tears welled up. "If you want me to go, I will. I won't be back, not tomorrow and not in fourteen years. My heart's been on my sleeve so long, it's getting frayed around the edges. I know what this must seem to you. I know what you think of me, but I just want to talk."

"Erin, it's three o'clock in the morning, I can't even put a sentence together."

"You listen, I'll talk. That's the way it's been most of the time anyway." He smiled and turned off the light, and while she sighed he worked himself from his clothes, leaving on underwear and adding a full set of pajamas. "Don't get any ideas, I'm even too tired for that," he said as he slid under the covers, staying on his side of the bed.

They lay side by side for a moment while Erin collected her thoughts, but it was Kevin who spoke. "You wouldn't by any chance, know something about the slightly faded rose over there on my dresser?"

"I'm courting you," she said glumly. "You think sex made a mess of all this because everything was new. You're afraid that I love you because we've been so intimate, but it's just the opposite. The intimacy came from loving you.

Kevin, loving you doesn't keep me from anything. I'm a country girl with the city an hour away. That's no different from the way I grew up. Loving you doesn't keep me from friends and experiences, it gives me someone to share them with. I wouldn't be here if I didn't know you felt the same; you've always loved me, always, Kevin. If you didn't, you would never have been so patient and gentle in the beginning and so damned miserable in the end."

"Erin, I keep trying to push you away, without destroying that spark, that fire."

"And do you feel better, Kevin? Are you relieved, darling? You're the cranberry baron marching around the bogs under a martyr's crown, making love as if each time must be the last—or worse, each time is a mistake. Even that's going to get better, because next time we're going to make love as if it's the beginning not the end."

"Erin!" His voice cracked on the word.

She sat up and propped her head in her open hand, her elbow deep in the pillow. "I'm your second chance, Kevin Branigan. I'm here to give you what you couldn't have when you were in your twenties. I'm here to make you feel that spark and know that fire. Come on, kid, there won't be many women in your life who drag you into the woods, refuse to take no for an answer and leave chocolates on your pillow even though you've sworn the love affair is over. You've met your match, and it's a perfect one."

"I knew it was you, of course. I think I got angry at first. You can't give so much, so openly, Erin. It's dangerous to keep coming back for more like some prize-fighter with more courage than sense. Why now, why just when we've gotten some grip on reality at least? Why start it all over again?"

"Because I want to get on with my life. This mourning and grief, and that's what it is, takes too much from both of us. It keeps me from my work, it keeps you from yours. You were meant for a woman who turns your life upside down. I want to be the one who hears what you've never shared. Do you think after all the prodding and murmuring and Swan Boat riding I've done with you, I'd let another woman just waltz in here and take over?

"Kevin," she whispered. "Do you think about my sleeping with someone else without it tearing at you? After all those moments, after all that gentle encouraging and practicing until I got it right, do you want me dragging somebody else into the woods?"

He laughed, but it ended in a sigh. "I try not to think about it."

"Well, I tried not thinking about it, too."

"Didn't seem to work, did it?" he murmured. As he spoke he moved, cradling her to him, shifting, no longer able to fight the fatigue. "You feel so good, Erin. You always felt so good. Maybe I thought if I never said I loved you, then it wouldn't be true. I love you enough to want the best for you."

Drowsiness settled over them. "I've found the best," she replied.

"Tomorrow," he replied. "This will seem clearer. It has to." He slid his arm around her ribs and whispered goodnight, molding her breast to his open hand like soft butter in a spoon.

They awoke slowly, as if drifting from a dream in unison. A yawn began in Kevin and pulled Erin from the last remnants of sleep as she filled her lungs and stretched against him. "You feel so good," he repeated as if they'd just quieted. "So good..."

"It's been a long time, Kevin," she replied. "Weeks of imagining I'd never be here again, never feel you stir the way you are now, the way you always do." She gasped softly as he slowly closed his arms across her back, raising his knee between her legs, against the bare skin to the cotton of her underwear. He lay with his face against her neck, his breathing even but rapid.

"You shouldn't have come here, Erin."

Eighteen
———

She turned around to face him, moving against and under the welcome pressure of his leg between hers. "What needs to be said, should be discussed downstairs," he tried.

"In a minute?" Her hands were never still.

"More than one."

Erin smiled. Kevin held her to him for long, quiet moments, saying nothing more than "Mmmm," as he savored the feel of her.

"Talk, remember?" she said as he unbuttoned the oversize pajama top.

He nodded, pushing the shirt roughly from her shoulders as if the weeks of denial and her week of *courting* had loosened the floodgates. "What you do to a person is inhuman," he groaned.

"I've had a very patient, sensuous, loving teacher."

He brushed himself out of his sleepwear. "You've called me a cantankerous, old bachelor before."

"With a heart as big as Wyoming."

He looked at her, puzzled.

She laughed softly. "Make love to me, Kevin, as if it were only the beginning."

"Heaven help me, Erin."

"Maybe heaven is. You're a good man who's given everything to those you love when they needed it. Surely there are rewards."

He laughed, deeply, contentedly, and looked down into her eyes as if he couldn't quite believe she was there. "My brothers'll be here soon."

"Any other excuses?" There might have been dozens but they were left unsaid as Kevin kissed her, crushing her to him as she caressed the small of his back.

Under the pressure of his mouth an unbearable tingling moved through her which made her hold him to her against the ache. Kevin slid his hands along her arms as if touching marble or silk and caressed each of her palms. The motion was repeated from her ankles up the insides of her thighs. "I woke up wanting you," he whispered hoarsely. She welcomed him, in reply.

A dog barked as they rocked, locked into the moment. The sun's reflection splintered through the windowpanes as a breeze rippled the bogs. This is love, she thought as Kevin touched her until she was mindless with the ache. She moved against him, saying nothing but his name, feeling him respond with every cry. With a rush that deepened her complexion and tightened her grip, the ache spread, shifting the torment to exquisite pleasure. Kevin's beard-roughened jaw grazed her cheek as she pulled him down, needing all of him against her. As he rocked, he gathered her up and the pleasure deepened. As if he'd been waiting for her, ecstasy rolled through them simultaneously in waves that peaked in a shower of sensation. They rode the crest and drifted together, sinking gradually back to the bright, autumn morning. Erin closed her eyes, dreading their parting.

"I've missed more than this," Kevin said. "The way we talked those hot nights after we'd made love, the way I felt then...the way I knew you felt. I knew your pleasure because I was the one who..." He shook his head. "Erin, it all happened before I could stop it. You wouldn't let me stop it then any more than you would this morning." He played with her hair and kissed her damp forehead. "You made me remember as you made me talk. The next thing I knew, I *wanted* to remember. I needed you to know what I felt. It just pulled you in deeper."

"Perhaps what you mean is that it pulled *you* in deeper, Kevin. It's easier to break off this affair with the excuse that you're all wrong for me than to take an honest look at what's happened. You're trusting someone with everything you've had control over until now. Kevin Branigan is being forced to take a chance. Love is risky business. I'm frightened, too."

He held her against him in comfortable silence. She longed to hear the words that would wrap the emotions into a tight little package. Instead of a heartfelt confession, however, she got an earful of the local weather as the clock radio snapped on.

"Good morning," Kevin said with a laugh. "We'd better do something about this. Everybody'll be here in no time."

"I'm staying for breakfast. I've got my clothes, the work is out there and, frankly, I don't care what your brothers think. Kevin, if you really believe nobody suspects anything, you're in for a bigger shock than the rose in your sports car. A man in love is as obvious as a child with chicken pox."

"And just as miserable," he added as he got up from the bed. As an afterthought, he turned and knelt over her as she sat up. "I want the truth right this minute. How did you mastermind all of this? What made you do it?"

"Sometimes even a child doesn't realize why he's itching and running a fever. He needs someone to tell him what's wrong, someone to tell him everybody gets it and he'll be just fine." She shook her loose hair over her shoulder and pulled Ryan's crumpled pajama top from the sheets. "There'll never be anyone else in your life like me, Kevin. After all this time you were acting as if you'd forgotten that. I thought I'd help you remember."

"You and a few others."

"Sky put the rose in the car for me and Holly turned down your quilt. Ryan drove me out here last night with some manly advice."

"Ryan!"

"I have quite a cheering section, probably because you've been so insufferable these past weeks." She muscled past him. "I'm surprised you haven't knocked out all the windows in the barn with your baseball bat."

"I'm giving it serious thought," he muttered.

"I could go on, Kevin, darling, but you're risking the chance of any number of Branigans charging up here momentarily and finding me stark naked in your bedroom." With that she went into the bathroom and showered.

Ryan and Sky arrived as she was cleaning up the breakfast dishes and Kevin was pulling on thick, wool socks. Sky went to his chair and mussed his hair. "So Kevin Branigan's been up to a few tricks of his own. You devil!"

"It's not too late to ship you back to Europe again," he muttered. "Ryan, if you say so much as one word, I'll call the police chief and get you your old job back. With any

uck at all the rest of the family will think Erin came over
ere with you two. Now, could we please get outside and
oncentrate on what has to be done?''

"Kevin, darling," Erin murmured as she picked up her
acket, "I've been doing that all along."

The temperature had risen to the sixties by the time the
family gathered. The children wrestled with the dogs and the
men pulled on their waders. Holly and Anne volunteered for
lunch detail since they had the youngsters in their charge.
The festive air and pressing deadline wove them together in
a heady combination of love and goals. Erin's heart sang.

The bogs lay flooded and shimmering between the
brothers' houses, the acreage closest to Kevin's already prepared. Millions of berries floated, waiting to be skimmed
and corralled onto the conveyor belt and up into the open
container truck. On the far side of the dike, the cranberries
were still submerged on the bushes. Kevin stood with his
family crew as jobs were delegated.

Matt, who was standing next to him, touched Erin's arm.
"Greg called you. His father's in town from L.A. and he
wants to get the two of you together over dinner at the Harvard Club. Talk shop *and* meet the old man." Matt arched
his eyebrows suggestively. "I said you'd be home tonight."

Kevin stopped his simultaneous conversation in midsentence, glowering at Erin and her roommate.

"Kevin?" Ryan said from the other side of him.

"Water reel," Kevin barked. "I said you and Sean take
the reels and get started. Do I have to repeat myself?" With
that, Kevin started off toward the bog with the floating
berries, rakes in tow.

Matt shrugged and climbed over the truck to supervise the
loading. Jody pulled on his waders. Kevin waded through
the shin-deep water to where Sky already stood; she nudged
him playfully. "Little testy this morning, aren't we?"

"Work to be done," Kevin replied. "Can't wait all day
As he spoke he watched Jody help Erin into waders. Sh
stood on the dike, feeling Kevin's stare, laughing neverth
less, as Jody adjusted the suspenders and the bib front an
then showed her how to handle the rake. "Hustle!"

Jody looked out at his brother. "Don't panic," he calle
back, taking Erin's hand and helping her down the sul
merged ramp which skirted the five-foot ditch at the edge c
the bog. The two of them made their way inside the corr
and formed a semicircle with Kevin, as Sky fed the con
veyor belt.

The harvesting process was slow, pleasant, manual labo
and over the hum of the belt's engine, Jody made conver
sation. "Erin, do you have much interest in classical mu
sic?"

She pushed the water, urging the berries forward. "Some
I've gotten over to Symphony Hall a couple of times, mostl
to hear the Pops in the spring."

"Would you like to hear some Haydn next Saturday
night? It's the opening concert for the Plymouth Philharmonic. We underwrite the performance so we have great
seats." He looked beyond her to Kevin. "Could she stay
here, again? We could make a day of it."

"That would be nice," Erin found herself saying. "Kevin,
would you mind if I used your hospitality once more so I can
go out with Jody? We never did have that date you set up
last summer. You'll be busy, probably never even know I'm
around."

The fair, Irish complexion was given to flushes in each of
the Branigans and as Erin watched, color seeped into Kevin's jaw and washed over the bridge of his nose. His expression was incredulous as he looked, first at Jody and then at
Erin. "That's enough," he cried, far louder than he'd intended. Matt turned off the engine; heads turned.

Kevin turned from those next to him to those at a distance. "Get back to work," he called. Nobody moved. Jody, I swear..."

"What?" the younger brother asked.

Kevin clenched his jaw, staring now at Erin. Without turning around he pointed behind him to the barn. Sky bucked as his hand came across her shoulder. "Erin O'Connor, every window over there is in jeopardy. I love you, I thought that was clear this morning." He lowered his voice.

Her eyes wide, Erin gave him her most innocent smile. "You never said anything."

It was as far as she got before he put a hand on each of her shoulders. "I'm saying it now. I love you, as much, maybe more than you love me."

"I thought so."

"Then we understand each other. When a woman loves a man, she doesn't go to the symphony with that man's brother. She doesn't want to meet another man's father as a prospective in-law. She probably shouldn't live with another man either, even if *he* were a brother, too." He put his head down on the rake handle.

Behind them the water reels stopped. Ryan and Sean came to the dike anticipating a problem. Matt was shrugging his shoulders to Drew. Kevin straightened up and looked deliberately from one brother to another then to each of the women on the lawn. "Okay," he called out. "I admit it. The rumors are true. I love her. I am in love with Erin Flynn O'Connor." He stopped abruptly, his expression a combination of pain and relief.

He turned sharply back to Erin. "You make me crazy," he muttered and then, as if more public confessions were beyond bearing, he scooped her into his arms.

"Kevin!" she cried as the water sluiced off her wader
berries and bits of leaves falling into the water. Around the
wolf whistles and catcalls rose from the family. The
cheered wildly as he plowed through the harvest, leaving
swirling, crimson wake.

At the ramp he tightened his grip and lifted her onto th
dike, but the moment her feet touched the earth she was u
again, rising on her toes to meet his lips. She threw her arm
around his neck and kissed him until he stopped fighting i

Kevin moved his hands from her wrists to her arms an
finally around her back. "I love you, Erin, I can't fight i
anymore. There's no peace without you. I can't sleep, I can'
concentrate." His voice was barely audible as the worl
around them dissolved. "You've ruined me for solitude
you've taken over all the empty spaces. Stay with me and fil
that big empty house. My God, I hate it when you go." His
embrace was bone crushing and even through the heavy
clothes and waders she felt the need, equally matched, to be
held. "I need you Erin, I don't want to share this with anyone but you." He blinked hard and looked over her head at
the blue October, Branigan sky. "Marry me, make this all
work. Say *yes*."

Against her chest she felt his breath catch, but he was
laughing. "This time say *yes*. It's all I want to hear."

She pushed him away, far enough to look into his shining eyes. "It's all I've been saying since the start. Yes. Yes,
yes, yes. Of course we can make it work. I love you, I've always loved you."

Behind them the cheering dwindled to applause and as
they broke from a final kiss, Kevin and Erin turned, arm in
arm to the rest of the Branigans. Five men and three women
were staring.

The couple walked to the edge of the bog. "Don't you
have work to do?" Kevin called to them.

"Don't you have some explanation?" Ryan called back.
Erin grinned and cupped her hands around her mouth.
He asked me," she called. The cheering rose again and
ver the noise Kevin, too, cupped his hands.
"She said *yes*!"

*   *   *   *   *

ATTRACTIVE, SPACE SAVING BOOK RACK

Display your most prized novels on this handsome and sturdy book rack. The hand-rubbed walnut finish will blend into your library decor with quiet elegance, providing a practical organizer for your favorite hard-or soft-covered books.

Only $9.95

Approximately 16" x 8" when assembled

Assembles in seconds!

To order, rush your name, address and zip code, along with a check or money order for $10.70* ($9.95 plus 75¢ postage and handling) payable to *Silhouette Books.*

Silhouette Books
Book Rack Offer
901 Fuhrmann Blvd.
P.O. Box 1396
Buffalo, NY 14269-1396

Offer not available in Canada.

BKR-2A

*New York and Iowa residents add appropriate sales tax.

Silhouette Intimate Moments

Starting in October...

SHADOWS ON THE NILE

by

Heather Graham Pozzessere

A romantic short story in six installments from best-selling author Heather Graham Pozzessere.

The first chapter of this intriguing romance will appear in all Silhouette titles published in October. The remaining five chapters will appear, one per month, in Silhouette Intimate Moments' titles for November through March '88.

Don't miss "*Shadows on the Nile*"—a special treat, coming to you in October. Only from Silhouette Books.

Be There!

IMSS-1

Silhouette Desire

ANOTHER BRIDE FOR A BRANIGAN BROTHER!
Available September 1987
by
Leslie Davis Guccione

The cranberry-growing Branigan brothers are at it again! In #376 *Something in Common*, feisty Erin O'Connor teaches Kevin, the eldest of the six brothers, a much-needed lesson in love.

It all began in October 1986 with Drew Branigan's crusade to make Holly Bancroft see the error of her ways in #311 *Bittersweet Harvest*.

Then Drew's hoodlum-turned-cop younger brother, Ryan, gets his chance to win his childhood sweetheart in #353 *Still Waters*, published May 1987.

Don't miss out on any of the Branigan family fun, coming to you in the Silhouette Desire line.
